She wished they could go back in time, back to those two kids who had fallen in love, and try again.

Tell her younger self to be wise and give Carter another chance. But it was too late now because she could never ask him to leave their tribe and she was too ashamed to stay.

Despite her reservations, her heart hammered in giddy excitement and her skin flushed.

Focus. You're in real trouble and this man doesn't want a woman who walked away from her family.

Carter had loved her. But he loved his people and his place among them more. He was not leaving and she was not staying. There was no future for them. Only more pain.

"Thank you for saving us back there," she said.

"I didn't get us out. I'd have been cuffed to the handgrip in a smoldering wreck if not for you."

He'd been the reason they had a chance to get out of that SUV and they both knew it.

TURQUOISE GUARDIAN

JENNA KERNAN

———

HARLEQUIN INTRIGUE®

For Ann Leslie Tuttle with many thanks for sharing her expertise, invaluable critical eye and friendship for more than a decade.

And for Jim, always.

ISBN-13: 978-1-335-72073-3

Turquoise Guardian

Copyright © 2016 by Jeannette H. Monaco

Recycling programs for this product may not exist in your area.

This edition published by arrangement with Harlequin Books S.A.

For questions and comments about the quality of this book, please contact us at CustomerService@Harlequin.com.

® and TM are trademarks of Harlequin Enterprises Limited or its corporate affiliates. Trademarks indicated with ® are registered in the United States Patent and Trademark Office, the Canadian Intellectual Property Office and in other countries.

Printed in U.S.A.

www.Harlequin.com

Jenna Kernan has penned over two dozen novels and has received two RITA® Award nominations. Jenna is every bit as adventurous as her heroines. Her hobbies include recreational gold prospecting, scuba diving and gem hunting. Jenna grew up in the Catskills and currently lives in the Hudson Valley of New York State with her husband. Follow Jenna on Twitter, @jennakernan, on Facebook or at jennakernan.com.

Books by Jenna Kernan

Harlequin Intrigue

Apache Protectors: Tribal Thunder

Turquoise Guardian

Apache Protectors

Shadow Wolf
Hunter Moon
Tribal Law
Native Born

Harlequin Historical

Gold Rush Groom
The Texas Ranger's Daughter
Wild West Christmas
A Family for the Rancher
Running Wolf

Harlequin Nocturne

Dream Stalker
Ghost Stalker
Soul Whisperer
Beauty's Beast
The Vampire's Wolf
The Shifter's Choice

Visit the Author Profile page at Harlequin.com for more titles.

CAST OF CHARACTERS

Carter Bear Den—Former US Marine, member of the Turquoise Guardians and assumed leader of the four warriors known as Tribal Thunder.

Amber Kitcheyan—Former Turquoise Canyon Apache tribe member and once engaged to Carter Bear Den.

Jack Bear Den—A detective with the tribal police, a Turquoise Guardian and Carter's fraternal twin.

Eli Casey—Police officer in Darabee and always first man at the scene.

Orson Casey—Ex-con brother of Eli Casey and member of several extremist groups.

Larry Seally Kirkson—Apache tribe member, hunting guide and part-time logger.

Kenshaw Little Falcon—The tribe's medicine man and a spiritual leader with strong ties to community, tradition and the land.

Dylan Tehauno—A Turquoise Warrior and Carter's best friend.

Ray Strong—A Turquoise Warrior with a reputation for making bad choices.

Jefferson Rowe—Chief of police in the larger neighboring community of Darabee.

Kurt Bear Den—Carter's younger brother and member of the tribe's police force.

Thomas Bear Den—The youngest of the Bear Den boys and a Shadow Wolf working for Immigration and Customs Enforcement.

Prologue

The idea of murdering seven innocent people should have sickened Ovidio Natal Sanchez. Instead he felt a grim anticipation. These people were responsible for causing that festering wound on the earth. He only wished he had been given free rein to kill as many as possible. But he was a loyal member of BEAR, and he would carry out his mission, with pleasure. He sat in a nondescript van before the loading dock of the Lilac Copper Mine, holding an automatic weapon with the safety switched off.

His driver's phone chimed, signaling a text.

"They're all in," he said.

"Give them twenty minutes to get to their desks," said Ovidio.

His driver cast him a look.

"I don't want to miss one who went for coffee."

His driver's sigh was audible, but he said no more, granting Ovidio a few more seconds to savor the moment.

His organization had supplied everything he needed: maps, head shots of each target, transportation and the automatic weapon he would use to kill every living soul in the procurement office of the Lilac Copper Mine. He didn't know why. He didn't care why. He just knew when and how.

Today. By his hand.

The twenty minutes ticked by.

A smile curled his lips. The next hole that went in the earth would be for their caskets.

"I'm signaling our man," said his driver and began texting.

The van was parked at the receiving bays.

Ovidio had worked protection for his boss for years. Even had to kill a few people. But nothing like this. He licked the salt from his upper lip.

In life, he believed, people mostly got what they deserved. Today was the exception. These people deserved worse. If it were up to him, he'd tie the owners of this monstrous mile-deep pit with their own blasting cord and toss them in with the next load of explosives. But his leader said they had bigger fish to fry. This time they'd make a statement that would not be buried on page six. One that the whole world would feel, and know that the earth mattered. That people couldn't keep assaulting the earth with impunity and that...

"You ready?" asked his driver.

The loading door was opening. He needed to focus.

"There he is," said his driver and looked expectantly at Ovidio. "Hurry up."

He wondered if his driver would really be here when he came out or would just leave him. But leaving him was dangerous. He might tell what he knew. He never would, of course. He believed too deeply in their cause. Still, they might kill him. Shoot him the instant he came out that door. He didn't care. At least his death would matter and they'd never forget him here in this miserable mining town.

Ovidio checked his weapon and slipped from the

van. His body tingled as he mounted the five cement stairs that took him from the bright sunlight to the shadows of the loading bay, the sensation reminding him of sexual arousal. Oh, yeah. He was getting off on it because he knew he was on surveillance now. And what would they do with only their rent-a-cops and crappy wire fences for protection?

How long until they spotted him? In the hall? After the first shots?

His conspirator stood holding the door and, as he passed through, relayed a message.

"Ibsen called in sick."

"Address?"

The man passed him a sheet of paper. Now Ovidio had to get out of here alive to get Ibsen.

Somehow Ovidio thought after he told his commander at BEAR about the discovery made by the new purchasing clerk, Ibsen would know what was coming. Unfortunately it was too late to abort. Besides there was no way of knowing who in the office the clerk had spoken to about her discovery.

Ovidio stalked into the corridor. Today he would write his convictions in blood.

Ovidio continued toward his goal, inhaling the scent of machine oil coming from the automatic rifle heavy in his hands. He thought of the memorials and the anniversaries of the legacy he was about to leave behind. But this wasn't his legacy. The removal of men who violated the earth—that was his legacy.

Chapter One

"I'll be back soon." Amber Kitcheyan stowed the last of the receiving slips she needed signed by her boss in her satchel as she spoke to their receptionist. Then she headed out from the receiving department in the Lilac Copper Mine's administration building where she was a receiving clerk.

Their squat building sat at ground level perched over the thousand-foot cavity, which was the active open-pit copper mine. Below them, a constant stream of enormous mining dump trucks wove up the precarious roads, hauling ore to the stamp mills in Cherub. The pit covered two-hundred acres and the tailing piles covered even more ground. To Amber, it looked like a crater left by some absent meteor.

Amber always left by the loading dock as it was closer to the parking area. She stopped in the restroom for just a moment. Too much coffee, she thought as she left the stall. She glanced at her reflection in the mirror as she washed her hands, checking that her long black hair was all tucked neatly up in a tight coil. She wore nothing in particular that marked her Apache lineage because her face structure and skin tone did that adequately. The human resources had been happy to tick the box indicating they had hired a minority. She didn't care. A job was a job and this one paid better than the last.

But she missed her tribe and her sisters. And wished…no, she wasn't going there. Not today.

Amber tugged at the ill-fitting blazer she'd purchased used with the white blouse she wore twice a week. She slung the stylish satchel on her shoulder and headed out into the hall.

On the loading dock she paused to slip her sunglasses out of her bag and swept a hand over her hair. February in Lilac was a good twenty degrees warmer than the Turquoise Canyon Apache Indian Reservation where she had grown up. She longed for a cool breeze off the river but now wasn't the time to be feeling homesick. She stopped to find her keys. Amber didn't like to bother her boss, Mr. Ibsen, at home, especially when he was sick. But as a clerk she couldn't sign for a delivery this big. So she'd just slip out there, get his signature on the receiving slips and be back before the truck was unloaded.

She had called from the office and got his voice mail and followed up with an email. It worried her that he had not replied to either and that, on the day after she mentioned the problem she'd spotted on the receipts to her boss, he was absent. And he knew they expected another delivery truck today.

She could have them signed by Joseph Minden in finance, but the one time her boss had been absent for a delivery, she'd done just that and her boss had lost it. She'd never seen veins stick out of a man's neck like that before.

Minden was their CPO, Chief Procurement Officer, and Mr. Ibsen's supervisor. Later in the day, Mr. Ibsen had explained to her about chain of command and threatened to fire her if she did something like that again.

Then yesterday he had also shouted at her to get back to work. Amber was on shaky ground here, and she needed this job, what with the seemingly endless debt she was trying to pay down.

She couldn't afford to screw this up.

She'd only been here a month and was still getting used to the copper mine's policies. But she would not make that mistake twice because she needed this job for at least the next six months. Then the loan would be finished, and she could go home, if she wanted. The pit of her stomach knotted at the thought as mixed emotions flooded in.

"Not now," she whispered to herself and strode across the loading dock. The Arizona sky glowed a crystal blue, and the sun warmed the concrete pad beneath her feet. The temperature would rise rapidly, she knew, and then drop with the sun.

She glanced at the deep navy van illegally parked before the receiving bay, then back at the sign that indicated parking there was prohibited. The driver had shaggy blond hair poking out from beneath his ball cap like straw. She cast him a disapproving look, and he leaned forward over the wheel to glare right back.

Amber descended the steps in a rapid gait, making a beeline for her vehicle, which was small, ugly, used and paid for. She didn't do leases. She paid cash or did without.

As she drove out of the lot, Amber glanced back at the van still illegally parked, and then turned onto the road that would lead her through the high chain-link fencing and off the copper mine's property.

CARTER BEAR DEN'S first sign of trouble at the mine came in the form of a yelp from the security guard seated at the lobby reception desk. The guard's eyes were glued to the monitor on his desk, showing a series of images from various security cameras. Carter leaned in to see what had made the man blanch.

Carter had a message to deliver. He didn't like it, but he was duty bound to see that Amber Kitcheyan received the letter. It had been given to him by Kenshaw Little Falcon, the head of the Turquoise Guardians, his medicine society and a tribal shaman.

Now, standing beside the security desk and the uniformed boy they had hired to check in visitors, Carter looked at the monitor that showed a masked gunman making steady progress along an empty corridor, and he stopped thinking and wondering. This time he saw the face of danger before it was too late.

Amber was in this building.

The security officer stood now, one hand on his pistol grip and the other reaching for the phone seeming uncertain as to which to use.

Carter had no such trouble. As a former US Marine with three tours of duty, he knew what he needed to do. Protect Amber.

The digital feed displayed a view of an office where the masked gunman proceeded past a fallen woman toward the cubbies tucked directly behind the receptionist's station.

"Where is that?"

"Purchasing," rasped the guard.

From the security guard's radio came a call to lock down. On the other monitors people scurried about, fleeing the halls for the closest cover.

Carter retrieved his Tribal ID from the high counter and tucked it in his open wallet as the shooting started, the burring sound of an automatic rifle blast unmistakable and close.

For just an instant, Carter was back there in Iraq with his brother and Ray and Dylan and Hatch. The next instant he was drenched with sweat and running.

Suddenly delivering his message came second to keeping Amber alive. Had Little Falcon known what was about to transpire?

The stabbing fear over Amber's safety took him by surprise. He'd been so sure he was over her. So why was he running into gunfire?

Although he now moved forward with the stealth of his ancestry bolstered by the training of the US Marines, the stillness in the corridor was unnerving. It had the eerie quiet of a deadly game of hide-and-seek. Everyone was hiding except for him and the killer.

From down the corridor he heard a bang, like the sound of a heavy door slamming shut. He ran toward the sound, the light tread of his cowboy boots a whisper on the carpeted hallway.

He saw the blood trail as soon as he rounded the corner. It led from an office that read *Purchasing* upon the door. The gunman's boot prints were there in blood leaving the scene, dark stains on the industrial carpeting.

Amber's office, he realized. For an instant he was too terrified of what he might find to go inside. Was it the same as Iraq? Was it already too late?

He held his breath and stepped across the threshold. The calm sending his flesh crawling. He moved from one body to the next, checking for signs of life and the face that still visited his dreams.

Everyone in the outer office was dead. He moved to the two private offices. The man in the first was gone, shot cleanly through the forehead. In the next office he was greeted by the sight of dark legs, sprawled at an unnatural angle. One moved.

Carter was at her side in an instant, sweeping away the dark hair that covered her face. She was breathing, but she was not Amber. Her eyes fluttered open and flashed to his.

"Rest. Help is coming," he said, feeling his gut twist in sympathy.

He could tell by her sadness and the tears in her eyes that she saw death coming.

"Amber?" he whispered.

"She left. When the shooter spotted her empty cubicle, he said he would find her."

His heart gave a leap and hammered now, hitting his ribs so hard and fast it hurt.

"Where is she?"

"Left. Harvey Ibsen's home. Paperwork. Oh, it hurts. My kids. Tell them I'm sorry. That I love them." Her eyes fluttered shut.

Someone entered the office.

"Security!"

"In here," Carter called.

A moment later a man in a gray uniform shirt and black pants appeared in the doorway. His gun drawn.

Carter lifted his hands. "Unarmed."

The man aimed his weapon. Carter didn't have time to get shot.

"EMTs on the way?" he asked.

The man nodded, his face ashen.

"Come put pressure on this."

He did, tucking away his weapon and kneeling beside Carter before placing a large hand on the folded fabric over the woman's abdomen.

"You know a guy called Harvey Ibsen?" Carter asked.

"Yeah. He works here."

"Where does he live?"

"I don't know. In town, I guess. Who are you?"

"Friend of Amber Kitcheyan." Friend? Once he had planned to make her his wife.

"Yeah?"

Carter was already on his feet. He pointed at the woman. "She wants her kids to know she's sorry to leave them and that she loves them."

The security officer blanched. Carter stepped away.

"Hey, you can't leave."

Carter ignored him. If the shooter was after Amber, he had to go. Now.

"She also said that the shooter was looking for Amber. Send police to Ibsen's home. I think he's heading there."

The man's eyes widened and he lifted his radio.

"Call Amber's cell. Warn her," said Carter.

"She doesn't own a mobile. Or at least that's what she told me." The security officer's eyes slid away.

Carter groaned. Of course she didn't. That would have made the necessity of him delivering this message superfluous. He headed out, following the ghastly bloody footprints. His phone supplied an address for a Harvey Ibsen, and his maps program gave him the route.

Ibsen didn't live in Lilac. According to Carter's search engine, he lived in Epitaph, the tourist town fifteen miles north of here. The name, once a joke for the number of murders committed during the mining town's heyday, now seemed a grim omen.

Carter swung up behind the wheel of his F-150 pickup. Amber's boss was out the very day this happened. A coincidence that was just too perfect in timing. Luck. Fate. Or something else?

He didn't know, but he had a sour taste in his mouth.

Chapter Two

Carter headed out, turning away from the town of Lilac, named not for the color of the rock, but the name of the man who decided to crush the poor-quality copper ore in a stamp mill and make the low-grade ore profitable.

En route to Epitaph, he phoned his twin brother, Jack, a detective with the tribal police back home on Turquoise Canyon Reservation, and filled him in.

"We have no jurisdiction outside of the tribe," said Jack. "You're practically in Mexico."

Actually he was thirty miles from there and heading north.

"See what you can find out. Tell them that Amber is a member of our tribe."

"She left the tribe, Carter."

"They don't know that." Carter reined himself in. He wouldn't lose his temper or shout at his brother.

There was a pause.

"Ibsen lives in a small housing development in Epitaph. You need the address?"

"Got it."

"Okay. I'll call border patrol. They might have a

checkpoint set up along that stretch. What is the shooter driving?"

"Don't know."

"Do you want me to call the others?"

He meant the members of Tribal Thunder, the warriors of the Turquoise Guardian medicine society. The ones charged with protecting their ancestral land and people from all enemies.

"Call Little Falcon."

"I'll call Tommy, as well. He's down there somewhere. Maybe he can help," said Jack.

Tommy was their brother. At twenty-six he had scored a spot on the elite all–Native American trackers under Immigration and Customs Enforcement, known as the Shadow Wolves, and had been down there on and off for two years. Carter supposed not all the Bear Dens could be Hot Shots. A Hot Shot was a member of an elite team of firefighters flown into battle forest fires, and the Turquoise Canyon Hot Shot team was one of the most respected and sought after in the nation, a reputation they had earned with hard, dangerous work. He and the other members of his former US Marine outfit all missed the buzz of adrenaline, and so had joined the most dangerous job they could find as a substitute.

"Great. Gotta go."

"Be careful," said Jack.

Carter hung up and slipped the phone into his front pocket. Amber still didn't have a cellular phone. She hadn't owned one the last time he'd seen her either.

"Please, don't let that be the last time," he whispered and pressed the accelerator.

AMBER HUMMED A tune about being happy as she rolled along. The fifteen mile drive out to Harvey Ibsen's was uneventful, and the scenery was lovely, so different than Turquoise Canyon. The roads were well maintained and flat as Kansas. She whizzed past dry yellow grass dotted with silver-green yucca and woolly cholla cacti with spines that looked like fur.

There were no cacti up on Turquoise Canyon. Here the planes stretched out wide-open to the snowcapped Huachuca Mountains to her right and the rockier Dragoon Mountains to her left where Apache warrior, Cochise, once kept a stronghold. The mountain ranges here did not look like those near Black Mountain, but at least the Huachucas got snow.

She missed home, still, after all this time. The Turquoise Canyon Apache Indian Reservation gleaned its name from the exposed vein of blue stone on Turquoise Ridge. Her tribe was a conglomeration of many Tonto Apache people, the losers in the wars against the Anglos, relocated twice until finally reclaiming a small portion of their lands. And the Turquoise Canyon Apache tribe had timber, turquoise and decorative red sandstone. They also had the best Hot Shots in the world. She supposed the warrior spirit lived on in the men of her tribe who now flew all over the West to battle forest fires.

Carter was a Hot Shot. Her smile faded, and her heart ached at the thought of the man she'd once loved.

She caught movement behind her and saw a dark vehicle closing fast. She held her steady pace and frowned as she recognized the van a moment before it swerved to the opposite lane and zoomed past her. It was the same illegally parked van at the loading dock, or so she thought. Her brow wrinkled as the vehicle vanished in the distance. How fast had that van been going to make her look like she was driving backward?

Amber continued on but now with a sense of disquiet that niggled at her. She signaled her turn, though there was no one behind her.

She checked the numbers on the houses she passed. She had been here once on a similar mission, but the houses were very alike; her boss's home had solar panels, so she studied the roofs as she passed. When she arrived at number nineteen, she slowed before the house. Harvey's hybrid vehicle was parked in the drive. That's when she saw the familiar blue van was already on the corner. She slipped the car into Park, instead of electing to turn into Harvey's ample drive. Something felt wrong, and she leaned forward to stare out the passenger window. Something about that van gave her the creeps.

Amber had to be back soon because the shipment was being unloaded as she sat there dithering. As she turned off the engine, she resisted the urge to start the engine back up again. The last of the air-conditioning dissipated, forcing a decision. She was being ridiculous.

She grabbed her satchel and then the car's door handle, stepping out into the street. She took a moment to tug down her cream-colored jacket and smooth her dark slacks. Then she closed the door.

She'd just made it up the drive when she heard a male voice speaking from inside the house. The tone was so strained that she did not at first recognize it, but then the strangled timbre became familiar, a version of Harvey Ibsen's speech that she recognized but had never before heard.

"I told you everything. I reported it, for God's sake. I told you we had a problem."

There was a pause and then Ibsen again, whimpering, begging now.

"Oh, but I'm one of you. I'm the one who—"

The sound of a gunshot brought Amber up straight. Her eyes widened, her jaw clamped, and her grip on the shoulder strap of her satchel tightened. Her mind struggled to catch up with her body as her heart rate leaped and a sheen of sweat covered her skin.

The second shot set her in motion. She spun and ran back to the curb. She dropped her satchel in the street beside her car as she crouched.

Her breath now came so fast she choked on the dry air. Heat from the pavement radiated up through the soles of her shoes, and her image reflected off the metal of her door panel before her. She could see herself in the white paint—all wide eyes and cowering form.

She glanced toward the van, perpendicular to her hiding place, and inched back out of sight, dragging her leather bag along the road as she moved away from the house. She ended up behind her rear bumper as she heard the sound of footfalls crunching on the ornamental stone. She peeked up over the trunk.

He held a long black rifle in his hand, and his head was turned toward her car, the one that he likely knew had not been there when he entered Ibsen's home. He looked directly at her and she at him. They made eye contact for one endless second and then another.

His step faltered as he changed direction, raising the rifle stock to his shoulder as he headed for her at a quick march.

Chapter Three

Carter took the turn too fast, the wheels of his truck screeching in protest. This was the street. Where was Amber? And then he saw her. The car. The shooter. All at once.

Amber cowered beside the rear bumper of a rust bucket of a car that looked as substantial as an aluminum can. The dark blue van parked on the adjoining cross street looked right as a getaway vehicle. Before the house stood a single male, forties to fifties, dressed in jeans and an olive green windbreaker, an assault rifle lifted to his shoulder. His jaw was large and dark with stubble. Carter saw brown hair, a broad nose, a down-turned mouth and square forehead. Was this the man who had killed all those people at the copper mine? The gunman swung the rifle in Carter's direction as Carter's truck screeched to a halt beside Amber. He had expected her to open the door, but she didn't. Didn't wait for him to shout directions either.

Instead, Amber vaulted into the bed of his pickup and rolled as Carter accelerated. The spray of bullets peppered his tailgate as he turned away from the van. Behind him, the gunman stood in the road for a moment, then lowered his rifle and ran toward the van.

It wasn't over. He felt it in the pit of his stomach.

Amber pounded on the small sliding glass window that separated the cab from the truck bed. He swiped the window open and glanced back at her. She stared at him with wide eyes.

"You," she said.

He cast her a half smile and returned his focus to the road which was complicated by the distraction of Amber slithering through the narrow opening with the undulating ability of a belly dancer.

"You hurt?" he asked.

"No." Amber looked over her shoulder out the back. "He killed him."

"Ibsen?"

"Yes. I think so. I heard my boss… I heard shots. Maybe we should go back."

"No. Call 911."

"No phone."

"I'm buying you a phone."

"No, you are not."

He didn't have time to argue with her now. So he drew out his phone and passed it to her. She called the emergency number and gave them the address and situation. Her voice hardly wavered at all, but she kept her opposite hand pressed to her forehead as she spoke.

When she finished, she relaxed her hand, and his phone dropped limply into her lap. Suddenly she stiffened.

"My satchel!" She half turned in her seat. "I left it in the road."

"Forget it."

She pivoted back to place. "The packing slips. I'm responsible. They're gone," she said.

She settled in the seat beside him, her brow furrowed.

"Did you get a look at the one with the rifle?" asked Carter.

"What? Oh, yes. A good one."

"Driver?"

"Yeah."

"Think about them. Every detail."

"Are they coming?" Amber glanced back through the rear window at the road behind them.

"Not sure."

She gripped his forearm with both hands tight. The scar tissue tugged, and he winced. Who would have thought such a small woman would be so strong?

He scanned her worried face, taking in the changes, looking past the Anglo clothing and prim bun to the loose tendril of black silk caressing her jaw and falling away before her pointed chin. Her cheeks held a flush, and her dark eyes glimmered from beneath thick lashes, her eyes so black he could not see the pupils of her eyes. Her mouth, oh that mouth, pink and alluring with the small crescent scar cutting through the upper lip. That threadlike blemish had appeared while he was away on his first tour.

He turned back to the road. Beautiful, he decided, still and always the most beautiful woman in the world.

"How did you know where I was?" she asked.

"I was at the mine."

"But why are you here?"

There was no time for that now.

"There's been a shooting at the copper mine," he said.

He made another turn.

"What?"

He debated only an instant and then told her everything.

"Everyone in my office?" she whispered. "Are you sure?"

"Looked like it."

Amber covered her face and wept. The urge to shield her from the pain surged inside him. But driving at top speeds he could not even loop an arm around her shoulders as she cried.

Suddenly, she lifted her head and stared at him with deep dark eyes glimmering with pain. Her pointed chin trembled, and her tempting pink lips were parted in surprise. He felt a familiar tug at his heart. They'd been so good together.

He forced his gaze away.

"That's why you wanted me to remember what I saw," she said. "You think it's the same man."

"I do."

He wondered if, instead of asking her to remember, he should tell her to forget. But it was too late. They'd seen the shooter. She'd seen the driver. They were involved.

She righted herself in the seat and closed her eyes. Then she lifted his phone, and dictated every detail she could remember into a text. The sound of her voice still stirred him.

When she finished sending the text she returned his phone.

"Who did you text that to?"

"Your brother Jack."

His phone chimed as Jack sent back a question mark.

"That way, he has it, in case anything happens..."

"Nothing is going to happen. I got you."

She stared with a solemn expression that made her seem world-weary. He summoned a quick smile he hoped looked reassuring.

"Why are you in Lilac, Carter? Why today?"

He had that creepy sensation again. The one he felt when he learned that her boss was out today of all days. "I have a letter for you from Kenshaw Little Falcon."

"What?"

She shook her head, not understanding. "My uncle? Why would he send you?"

"He heads my medicine society now."

Did she ask why he had been chosen or why the message needed to be hand delivered?

"It's not from my father," she said, the statement really a question. He knew from her mother, Natalie Kitcheyan, that Amber had been back to visit, but she timed her appearances carefully so as not to encounter her dad, Manny Kitcheyan. She also never visited Carter again. After that last time, he couldn't blame her. But the truth that she'd moved on tugged at his heart.

Carter's phone rang. He fished it from his front pocket and passed it to her again.

"It's Jack," she said.

"Put him on speaker."

She did.

"Carter? Where are you?"

"I got her. But the guy was there at her boss's house. He's there, Jack, or he was. Two men. Dark blue Chevy van. Unmarked. Arizona plates."

"I'll call Arizona Highway Patrol. You safe?"

"For now. We're heading north."

"You guys clear?"

"Not sure. Any chance you can send Kurt down here for us?"

Carter was referring to their youngest brother, who was one of the pilots for the air ambulance transport team out of Darabee. In other words, Kurt might be able to get his hands on a helicopter.

"Either of you injured?"

He glanced at Amber, who was ashy and bleeding from the knees.

"If you need us to be, then, yes," said Carter.

"There's a hospital in Benson. Head there."

"En route," Carter said.

She disconnected and dropped the phone in his front breast pocket. She leaned in, wrapping her arms about his neck.

"You saved my life."

She stared at him in a look that made his stomach tug. Those big, beautiful eyes open and grateful to him. How he'd missed her. Nine years since she'd broken it off. Seven since he'd laid eyes on Amber, but his heart remembered. He knew because it banged against his rib cage. He was thirsty for her, as thirsty as the desert longing for the yearly floods. He forced his gaze back to the road. He couldn't do this again. The longing receded, replaced by the betrayal. Why did she leave her people?

Why did she leave him?

They could have worked it out. He'd been so stupid, and she'd been so stubborn. Blown to hell like that Humvee back in the Sandbox. No way to put back the pieces.

He glanced at her. Was there?

He looked in the rearview, spotted the van and stiffened. Amber followed the direction of his gaze, turning to stare through the rear window as Carter uttered a curse.

"It's them!" she cried.

Carter accelerated toward the highway. His truck was tough, eight cylinders, but the van was gaining on them. That didn't make any sense.

Amber spun in the seat, kneeling to look out the back.

"He's got that rifle out the window."

Carter pressed her head down. Then he brushed her off the seat so that she sprawled into the wheel well.

"Hold on." His truck might not be as fast as whatever engine they had in that van, but it had higher clearance and tires especially made for riding over rock and through soft sand. Carter braked and swerved from the highway into the shoulder and then veered off toward the cover of the trees that lined the San Pedro River. He braced as more bullets punctured a line of holes across his truck's rear gate. The rooster tail of dust and sand obscured the view of the van and hopefully them as a target from the shooter.

He needed both hands on the wheel to hold his course as they bumped across uneven ground and plowed through cacti; as the tall dry grass lashed against his bumper, sounding like heavy rain. He kept going, making for the river that he knew was dry in certain stretches for much of the year. Amber sat on the floorboards with one hand thrown across the seat and one on the glove box as she braced herself for the jolting ride through the thick chaparral to the flat stretch of the thirsty San Pedro. He had to get her out of here.

"Are they following us?" she called to be heard against the thudding of brush against the fender.

"Can't see," he said and lowered his chin as bursts of another desperate flight flashed through his mind like a thunderstorm.

Chapter Four

Carter made it to Benson and found the hospital. Jack had called in some chips, and Carter found Kurt waiting beside the air ambulance to transport him, Amber and a cooler full of blood to Darabee.

"Lucky you, there was a wreck on Route 88, and Darabee needs blood."

"Fatalities?"

"Not if we hurry. Hop in."

Kurt began his check as Carter helped Amber up and onto the gurney where the single paramedic waited. Carter wouldn't feel safe until the chopper was airborne. He hadn't felt this afraid since Iraq. But this time it wasn't his own survival he contemplated, but Amber's.

She lay on the cot beside the paramedic who had already cleaned up the abrasions on her knees and palms. She was wrapped in a blanket and still shivering. Carter scowled and adjusted the headset that allowed him to fill Kurt in on the details.

When they touched down, both the sheriff and his twin brother, Tribal Detective Jack Bear Den, were waiting. Behind them stood a member of Carter's tribal council, Wallace Tinnin, the chief of tribal police, and

Jefferson Rowe, the police chief from Darabee. Rowe was an Anglo, with dark curly hair that was receding and was clipped short at the sides. The deep parallel lines that flanked his mouth and the broad hooked nose did not quite balance his eyes, that were too widely set. Carter glanced to the parking lot beside the landing pad. He'd never seen so many police cars all in one place. Though he imagined the Lilac Copper Mine looked much the same about now.

"We have a welcoming party."

"Looks like a welcoming party from Grey Wolf," said Carter, referring to General George Crook by the name his people used. Crook had defeated the Tonto Apache with the help of Apache scouts, who were from a different tribe, back in 1883.

The slowing rotor blades kept back the welcoming committee temporarily, but Carter knew they needed to get onto sovereign land if he was to protect Amber.

The sheriff approached first. His brother was at the man's heels.

The sheriff shouted louder than necessary to be heard over the helicopter.

"Mr. Bear Den, I'm Sheriff Bill Taylor. I need you and Ms. Kitcheyan to come with us."

"Why?"

"She is a person of interest in an open investigation in Lilac," said the sheriff.

"Is she being charged with a crime?"

The sheriff shook his head, his hand going to his fleshy neck and then up to the bristle of hair that was all that remained after someone had taken clippers to his head.

"No. A witness."

"She's a member of our tribe and as such will be returning to Turquoise Canyon."

It was a lie. She wasn't a tribe member anymore and had no rights to protection from their people. But none of his tribe members corrected him. In fact, Jack had already opened the door to his tribal police unit and retrieved Amber, who was now flanked by tribal police officers and tribal officials.

Chief Rowe and his men watched as the sheriff took a step to move past Carter, but he shifted to intercept.

"I'll go with you," he said.

"I was told Ms. Kitcheyan was in need of medical attention."

"Delivered en route," said Carter.

Amber was now in the backseat of Jack's police car. Possession was now theirs. Carter placed two fingers above his brow and gave the sheriff a mock salute.

Then he trotted to his brother's unmarked car and slipped into the passenger seat, dragging the door shut with a satisfying snap.

"I hope Kurt isn't fired over this," said Jack.

"Me, too."

Police Chief Rowe stood beside Sheriff Taylor, who watched them with hands on hips as their chief of police, Wallace Tinnin, and tribal council member, Zach Gill, ran interference.

"They get the two in the van?" asked Carter, hoping like hell they caught the man responsible.

"Disappeared," said Jack Bear Den to Carter as he pulled out. "Arizona State Police and local law enforcement are still searching."

Carter glanced back at Amber, whose color had improved, but her blank expression and vacant stare worried him.

"She's going to have to talk to them," said Jack.

"They had video surveillance all over that building. They don't need her."

"Only witness, they said."

"I saw him, too," said Carter.

Jack lifted his brows. "But you I can protect."

"You can protect us both."

He gave a slow apologetic shake of his head. "It's just a matter of time, you know. They'll figure out that she's not one of us, and when they do, I can't stop them from taking her."

Carter's gut churned like a washing machine on agitate. Why had she done that—abandon her people and her poor parents? It was so stupid, pointless. He didn't understand, didn't think he could ever understand her actions. She had thrown them all away like a spoiled child.

"FBI is en route with requests to interview Amber." Jack glanced back at his passenger.

"No," said Carter.

"Carter, they're the Feds. I might be able to hold them off for twenty-four hours, but eventually they're coming to speak with her." Jack had correctly guessed that his brother did not want to speak to the FBI.

Carter glanced in the rearview at Amber. "You okay back there?"

She nodded, her eyes still unfocused. The one-thousand-yard stare, the marines called it. Shell shock, PTSD and usually a domain reserved to soldiers. She hadn't signed up for this.

"I'm taking you to the station. I can arrange to have one of my guys there when the FBI interviews you."

"Just get us home."

He drove them to the station and into the squad room where all nine of the officers from their tribe had desks. The chief's office was in the corner with windows looking out at the room. Jack's desk sat by the window with a view of the parking area and the road beyond.

Jack motioned to the chair beside his desk, the one reserved for witnesses and suspects. Which was Amber? Carter wondered.

"I need to use the bathroom," she said.

Jack gave her directions, and the brothers watched her exit to the hallway. Carter's brother gave him a once-over.

"You all right?" asked Jack.

Carter shook his head. "I used to think so."

His brother had served with him in Iraq. But after one tour, Jack had left the service. Now a detective, Jack was also a member of the Turquoise Guardians medicine society. Recently, Jack and Carter had also been inducted into Tribal Thunder. Their elite warrior band defending their people and their sacred land. Today Carter glimpsed the seriousness of their duty. How had Little Falcon known?

"Did you deliver the message?" asked Jack.

Carter patted his pocket. "Not yet."

"What do you think it is?" asked Jack.

"A warning, maybe." Carter met his brother's troubled gaze with one of his own. They didn't have to speak. Carter knew what Jack was thinking. He was also wondering if Kenshaw Little Falcon had prior knowledge of the mass shooting. The implications were staggering.

Jack pressed his mouth tight, clearly disagreeing. They were twins but did not resemble each other. Carter had features he thought were classic for the Tonto Apache people while Jack was built like a brick house. Carter wore his hair long and loose, but Jack clipped his dark brown hair short to avoid others seeing the natural curl, and had eyes that were closer to gray than brown. The differences didn't end there; he was three inches taller and had thick eyebrows that peaked in a way that made Jack look dangerous even when he was just hanging out. There had been questions when they were growing up. They didn't look like twins. They didn't even look like brothers, and Jack didn't look full-blood Apache. His skin was too light and his features too Anglo.

"The FBI has agents en route," said Jack.

"Don't let them take her, Jack," said Carter. If she left their land, Carter couldn't protect her. He knew it and Jack knew it.

Jack's scowl made him look even more intimidating than usual.

"Anything on Ibsen?" asked Carter.

"Head shot. Dead. My buddy on highway patrol says it looks like the same shooter as at the mine. Can't believe they missed the shooter twice. They've got helicopters, dogs, state and local cops, all searching and border patrol stopping everything heading south."

"Think they made it before the roadblocks?" asked Carter.

"Impossible."

"How do you think they got away?"

"Changed vehicles, split up. Likely they are within ten miles of where you saw them. They're doing a house-to-house in Ibsen's neighborhood."

"That will take some time," said Carter.

"I'm going to stick with Amber for a while," he said, and Jack's eyes narrowed, clearly not liking that plan.

"We should turn her over to the Feds."

Now Carter was scowling because that was not going to happen.

"It's my duty to protect her," said Carter.

He referred to his duty as a Turquoise Guardian, to protect their people and their sacred land.

"Guardians protect the people. She's no longer one of us."

Carter glared at his brother. "She's Apache. That's enough."

"Is it?"

"Yes."

Jack grimaced but said no more. He'd been there to pick up the pieces after Amber had left. Carter wasn't surprised that Jack was less than thrilled to have Amber back.

"Not again," said Jack.

Carter met his brother's warning with a glare of his own.

"She left. She didn't write. She didn't visit, not even after you were injured."

"I saw her after I came home from the hospital."

He hadn't told Jack. A rare omission that clearly surprised his twin.

"But she left again."

He couldn't deny that. But he knew he'd shown her the door. He'd been so hurt and angry. Yeager had still been MIA, and his days were filled with horror and hope. She'd asked about Hatch Yeager.

What do you care, Amber? Really. You disappear for two years, and then you think I owe you answers. I don't owe you a thing.

Carter met the disapproval in Jack's words with a steady stare. "Yeah, she left again after I threw her out."

Jack made a face. Carter couldn't tell what his brother thought about that.

"Maybe she's ready to come home," said Carter.

And maybe he was ready to let her. After today that was at least a possibility.

Jack shook his head. "Maybe she had no other choice."

Carter returned his attention to his brother, who raked a hand through his short brown hair. "What does that mean exactly?"

"She is a witness. They want her in federal custody."

"We both saw him. He was at her boss's house."

"And her boss is dead, too. Everyone is dead but Amber."

Carter didn't like the way Jack said that, as if this were all somehow her fault.

"Can't you just give her the message and forget about her?" Jack asked.

He'd never been able to forget about her. And oh, how he had tried. But even after all this time he wondered about what she was doing, thinking and if she missed him at all.

Could he?

He'd stayed away from her, but this was different. Because whether she would admit it or not, she needed him. He hated how much he needed that excuse to keep her close. He slipped both hands into his pockets, wishing he could give his brother the answer he wanted to hear and knowing he could not.

"I can't," said Carter.

Jack's mouth went tight.

"Carter, I'm telling you this as my brother. Let her go."

"Why?"

"Because Amber Kitcheyan isn't just a witness. She's also a suspect."

"How do you know that?"

"They told my boss. She should never have left the office with those papers. Makes her look guilty as hell."

"If she'd stayed, she'd be dead."

Jack glanced toward the window and swore.

Carter followed the direction of his brother's fixed attention. Amber was standing in the parking lot before the station alone.

Jack quirked a brow. "Still think she's innocent?"

Chapter Five

Amber stepped from the concrete building that included tribal headquarters and the tribal police station and breathed deep.

The air smelled so different here. She'd almost forgotten the crisp clean taste and the moisture. There was water here. Back in Lilac the earth was scorched and parched and thirsty. The dust was everywhere on everything and everyone. She didn't think she'd ever be clean again. Now she was. Standing here where she belonged.

Or had belonged.

Relinquished, they called it. Carter said it was irrevocable. She'd checked, of course, called the tribal council offices and asked if a tribe member who had relinquished their membership could reapply. The woman on the phone had been blunt. *No*, she had said. *The decision is not like a reversible blanket. Relinquishment is permanent and irrevocable.*

Amber added one more item to the list of things her father had stolen from her. And still he was her father and, as such, deserved to be honored. But not loved. He'd lost that along the way.

She thought of Carter, there when she needed him

most, and found herself shaking her head in astonishment. He had a message from her uncle, his shaman. She wondered if the message he carried was from her mother or her father.

She set her jaw and breathed, the cool air calming her. What would she do now? She could not go home to her family or stay here on tribal land. She could not bear to go back to Lilac, knowing what had happened. She shivered, afraid of the ghosts of all the ones she knew, torn from this world in such a brutal and cruel way.

Carter would know what to do. He was always so sure of himself. So sure he did not need to ask her what was true, he just moved forward. Omnipotent. But that wasn't love. It was some kind of possession. He had been too much like her father, and she would not have one more man controlling her. So she'd ended it. The decision had been hard but right. So why did it still hurt so much?

But oh, he was more handsome now than ever.

He had grown out his hair since his military service, and now he wore it loose and long, so it reached midway down his biceps, the strands shining blue-black in the sunlight as they'd flown in the chopper from Lilac. From her place lying on the gurney she could see him sitting beside his brother Kurt. Carter was a Hot Shot now, according to her sister Kay who sent her letters of the happenings on the Rez. Carter no longer wore his uniform, as he had the last time she had seen him. After three tours in the Middle East, he had been honorably discharged and relinquished the US Marine's uniform for a pair of snug jeans. He wore them cinched about his trim hips with an ornate red coral and turquoise buckle and a soft chambray shirt that showed his muscular form. She wondered if Carter had made the ornament himself because he was a talented silversmith.

A Subaru SUV pulled into the station. She noticed it because such foreign cars were uncommon up here on the Rez.

The black vehicle circled the lot and came to a stop at the curb before her. The driver put the car in Park but didn't shut down the engine. His passenger met Amber's gaze, and a smile quirked his lips as he exited the vehicle.

He wore a gray blazer and dark slacks. His ashy brown hair was trimmed and a shade lighter than the closely cut beard. He looked vaguely familiar, but she did not remember where or when she had seen him before.

"Ms. Kitcheyan? Will you please come with us, ma'am?" He had a strong Texas twang in his speech.

Amber stepped back. He reached in his blazer, and she saw his shoulder holster and the black butt of a pistol. He drew out a leather cover and opened the case, revealing an FBI shield.

"I'm Field Agent Muir with the FBI. My driver is Field Agent Leopold. We'll be taking you to the police station in Darabee to record your statements," said the agent.

Amber slipped back as her eyes shifted from the agents and then over her shoulder to the station door. It seemed impossibly far. She did not want to go with this man but thought running would be embarrassing.

She glanced at Muir, trying to understand the deep dread congealing in her stomach.

"If you'll step into the vehicle, ma'am." Muir extended a hand, indicating the rear seat that lay behind dark tinted windows. She shivered.

"I can't. They're waiting for me inside." She thumbed over her shoulder.

His smile looked more predatory than reassuring. And then it clicked. He wore a sports coat and pants. Not a suit. A sports jacket. She quirked a brow at that; it didn't seem right.

"Ma'am," he said again, his tone carrying a warning.

She didn't hear Carter arrive, but heard him a moment later and turned as he spoke.

"What's going on here?" Carter asked.

Muir showed his shield and repeated his request for Amber to step into the vehicle. His partner exited the driver's side and rounded the fender, his hand on the pistol clipped to his hip. He looked remarkably like Muir, with dark brown hair and aviator glasses that covered his eyes. He wore an ill-fitting black suit that puddled at his loafers.

Carter faced off with Muir.

"You're on tribal land," said Carter. "Sovereign land. You can't take her."

Muir and Leopold shared a silent look, and Carter spoke to her in Apache.

"These two aren't FBI."

Her eyes widened.

"You're not taking her," said Carter to Muir.

"Wanna bet?" said the driver, Leopold, drawing his weapon.

Horror immobilized Amber as the driver flicked off the safety and pointed the weapon at Carter. She moved to step before him, but he tugged her behind him.

"What's your name?" asked Muir.

"Carter Bear Den."

The men exchanged a second look. Leopold gave a lazy grin.

"Get in," said Muir. "Both of you."

They headed for the black Subaru SUV. Her eyes narrowed at the vehicle. Federal agents drove American-made vehicles. Impala, Taurus, Dodge Charger. She knew that from working a summer internship in Benson with Public Safety. What they didn't drive was foreign cars.

Carter was right. These two were not FBI.

She glanced to Carter, but he had his eyes on Muir who had now drawn his weapon.

"Get in," he said, motioning with his pistol.

Amber stepped up and into the SUV. Carter followed a moment later, and the door clicked shut behind them.

Carter spoke to Amber in Apache before either man got in the vehicle.

"Jack's watching from inside. He's seen them take us. We just have to stay alive until he can get to us."

Muir, or whatever his name was, got in first. He sat facing them, pistol pointed at Carter until the driver returned to the adjoining seat. Then they ordered Carter to lift his hands. The driver snapped a handcuff on one of Carter's wrists, threaded the chain through the handgrip fixed above his door before clipping the other cuff on his opposite wrist.

Amber swallowed and sank back in her seat trying to slow her heartbeat and think. Carter's face was grim, and she found no reassurance there.

Was there a tire iron or something? She glanced

about and found a car so spotless it belonged on a showroom floor.

They left the small lot and turned away from Darabee. That was bad, she thought, because to the south was only Red Rock Dam and the resort community of Turquoise Lake. Beyond that, down the highway which many called the Apache Trail, lay Phoenix.

The Subaru accelerated. Amber glanced at the digital speedometer, seeing that they had reached sixty, and the speed was still increasing. Outside her window the town of Pinyon Forks quickly gave way to pastureland dotted with the tribe's cattle. Past the open stretch, the mountains rose, thick with lush green Douglas fir and ponderosa pine that grew in abundance on their land. The tribe's land, she corrected. Not hers. Not anymore.

"What will they do to us?" she asked in Apache.

Carter's jaw set, and she had her answer. They were dead unless Jack found them first or she or Carter did something. Muir still sat with his back toward the windshield. Gun pointed at Carter.

"Attach your harness," Carter said in Apache.

"English," said the driver.

Amber drew a breath at the implication and reached for her safety belt. Whatever Carter planned, it involved a quick stop, maybe worse.

She fastened her seat belt that included a shoulder restraint. Carter, of course, could not do the same. She grabbed the armrest tight and waited. They were going so fast now, the seconds taking them farther and farther from Pinyon Forks.

Amber cleared her throat. Whatever Carter planned, it needed to be soon. But Muir kept his weapon raised and his attention on Carter.

"I'm going to be sick," she said.

Muir didn't bite. "Go ahead."

"Pull over, right now!" she shouted.

His eyes flicked to her, but the gun stayed pointed at Carter. Leopold did not even flinch but kept both hands on the wheel as Muir gave her a ferocious glare. In that moment of inattention, Carter clamped both hands around the handgrip, lifted one booted foot and kicked the driver with such force the man's head impacted the side window, cracking the glass.

Muir looked to his partner as Carter swung the pointed toe of his boot in his direction, the tip impacting Muir's eye socket. The man yelped and slapped his free hand over his eye, his pistol dipping out of Amber's line of vision.

Amber gasped at the violence of the attack and because the car was swerving now, leaving the highway at dizzying speeds.

The SUV veered across the center line as the driver's head lolled back in the seat, his hands dropping from the wheel. Muir lifted the pistol, and Amber lunged, leaving the shoulder restraint behind as she grabbed his arm with both hands and yanked up as the first shot went into the roof. Carter was now wrapping his legs around both the seat and passenger, trapping Muir's arm beside his head.

The SUV careened off the opposite shoulder and slid down the short embankment of grass. The jolting ride pressed Amber back into her seat. She grabbed at the door handle, but the door did not open. They bounced and jerked as the SUV thrashed through the long grass and weeds before breaking through the barbed wire fence. Her shoulder harness engaged, pinning her back in her seat and giving her an excellent view of the looming drop-off to the stream she knew ran cold and deep all year.

Amber screamed as the earth fell from beneath the front fender. The vehicle tipped to a right angle, and she glimpsed the rocky creek bed visible only because the snowpack had not yet melted with the spring runoff. An instant later, they hit the rocky bank. Her shoulder harness bit into her chest and squeezed her hips as the vehicle came to an abrupt halt at the same moment the front air bags inflated, throwing the unconscious driver and struggling passenger back. Their side air bag inflated, dislodging Carter. He was thrown sideways so hard it looked as if he were being hauled by a rope. He didn't move again.

The car's metal groaned, and the car fell back, the rear tires striking the bank behind them before coming to rest.

White powder filled the cab, and she couldn't see. Carter slumped beside her.

She shook him, screaming his name, then remembered it was dangerous to shake an accident victim. Then she shook him again. He didn't rouse.

White swirling dust began to settle on them like frost. The stillness deafened.

Chapter Six

Amber had to find the handcuff key. The guys in Benson had kept theirs in their wallets.

She released her seat belt. When she rolled her shoulder, she winced. Where was Muir's pistol?

First things first. She pushed the unconscious Muir forward into the deflating air bag and groped his back pockets, finding nothing. On her second try she located his wallet, in the front pocket of his blazer. She opened the worn brown leather and saw the license which read: Warren Cushing.

"Muir," she muttered and continued her search, locating the small handcuff key that most resembled a tiny luggage key.

How long until one of them woke up? She kept the wallet and used the key, more worried when Carter's hands dropped limply to his lap.

"Wake up, Carter!"

She tried the door again to the same end and then stared at the gap between the seats. It took only a moment to vault through the opening and lunge across the driver to reach the door release. The latch clicked, and she felt like crying in relief. Instead, she continued, head first out the door, clasping the armrest in passing to keep from sprawling on her face.

Once outside the SUV she spotted the driver's gun in a holster clipped on his belt. His face was a bloody mess as it seemed the air bag had broken his nose. She reached Leopold's gun, or whatever his name really was. His pistol went in the back of her waistband as if she were a gangster. She shut the door and hurried to the rear door where Carter slumped. Amber tugged Carter's door open and reached for him. He was heavy, and she realized she could tip him out, but then what?

She considered shooting both the unconscious impostors and dismissed the notion as she wrinkled her nose in disgust. She couldn't. She knew that much.

Her eyes caught the glint of something shiny, and she spotted the gun on the floor mat by Carter's feet. That pistol went in the front of her waistband. She could hear Warren Cushing groan as he started to regain consciousness.

She felt the pressure of time and the choice of leaving Carter or staying here with these two strangers. Well, she had the guns. What if Carter had been wrong and these men were really FBI and she and Carter had just attacked federal officers and wrecked a federal vehicle?

Amber's shoulders slumped. She wiped back tears and retrieved Carter's phone from his rear pocket. For the second time in one day she called for help, only this time she used Carter's favorites list to find and dial Jack Bear Den's cellular phone.

"Where are you?" asked Detective Bear Den.

She told him as best she could, not liking the high frantic quality of her voice. "We crashed the car. These men said they're FBI. Carter says they aren't, and one has an ID reading Warren Cushing, and he told me his name was Muir and—"

"Slow down," said Bear Den.

She grabbed a breath and swallowed, then started again. Her words came out a jumbled mess, and it took a moment for her to realize that Detective Bear Den was shouting her name. She stopped talking.

Then she noticed something, the meaning rising to fill her consciousness.

"I smell gas."

"What?" asked Bear Den. "Get him out of the vehicle!"

She thrust the phone in her pocket as the implications made her heart beat in her throat, choking out the stench. She gave Carter another sharp poke in the ribs. This time he groaned.

"Wake up, Carter," she said. "Wake up now!"

"Amber?" The voice came from the phone behind her. She ignored it to grasp Carter by the front of his soft chambray shirt.

She glanced about for cover. The closest thing was a large rock, to the left by the water, but it was too close and still half submerged in cold water. Next was a second outcropping along the bank that was maybe fifteen feet away. She glanced up the incline to the road above them, and it seemed impossibly steep.

She slung Carter's arm over her shoulders and tugged.

"Come on, Carter. Move!"

He groaned, and his arm tightened on her shoulders.

"Up, soldier! That's a direct order."

Another groan, but he swung his own legs out of the SUV and slid against her. His eyes fluttered.

"What happened?" He lifted a hand to his head.

"Later."

"Yeager. Get Yeager." Was he back in Iraq?

He slipped to a knee, and she had a sinking feeling that she'd never get him up again.

"Gas," he said.

"Yes. Let's go."

He used her as a crutch, and the weight nearly buckled her knees as they inched past the rear of the smoking Subaru and along the rocky bank of the stream. She threaded them under an overturned juniper, which had toppled from the bank above and now hung precariously before them.

They had come only twenty feet. But it would have to do because Carter dropped, carrying her to the ground with him. The juniper branches, still lush and loaded with the tight gray berries, fell like a curtain between them and the Subaru. She feared it would be little protection if the vehicle exploded. She got him to his side, and he groaned again.

"Like getting kicked by a horse," he muttered.

She picked up the sound of car doors closing and cowered. Was that help or the impostors coming after them?

CARTER'S EARS BUZZED as if he had just come from a rock concert. Dappled light filtered down on him with shards of sunlight so bright they seemed to slice the tissues of his eyes. His face hurt. His neck ached. He groaned.

"Quiet now," said a soft female voice, and a small hand pressed to his shoulder.

Who was that? He forced his eyes open. There, lying

beside him, was an unfamiliar woman who seemed to be covered in baby powder. For just a moment he thought he was dreaming as he looked on the sacred deity, Changing Woman, who brought rebirth to the land.

He lifted a hand to touch her cheek and found it warm and alive. Tear stains cut tracks through the white dust, revealing the soft brown skin beneath.

He glanced at his wrist, all red and raw skin, as if he'd been tied. Carter's gaze flicked back to hers.

"Amber?" he asked.

He had never seen her like this, disheveled and lost. What had happened?

He rocked his jaw, wondering who had hit him as he moved his hand from her face to his.

Amber took hold of his hands and squeezed. The ache now moved to his chest. Only she could make his heart ache and his body come alive with longing.

He'd loved her as a girl and lost her when she became a woman. He'd tried to forget her. Carter admitted now that he never could. Not this one, because she still owned a piece of his heart. He knew this because that piece now bled with longing for her. The woman who'd left him. But worse, she'd left her family and abandoned her people.

"Amber," he whispered, reaching up and cupping her cheek.

She smiled, and the powder on her face flaked at the corners of her eyes. Her hair was also powdered like George Washington's and tucked up in a knot at the back of her head. She used to wear it down so that it brushed the waistband of her jeans and his thighs when she sat astride him as they made love.

Why? Why had she thrown it all away? Their future—a life together here where they both belonged? Why was she ashamed of who and what she was?

Now her bun had shifted. Tendrils had escaped and hung about her powdered face. Her Anglo blazer was streaked with grime and sand, and she'd lost the top two buttons of her blouse. He reached up and cupped her chin, his thumb brushing that tiny crescent scar at her mouth.

"What happened?" he asked.

"Hush. Someone is here."

"Who?" he whispered and craned his neck in the direction she faced. That's when he realized he was lying against a wall of dirt behind a fast-running stream. The sun that hit them full in the face did not touch the opposite bank. Afternoon then or morning. He tried to make sense of his surroundings.

It all came back to him, up to and including the air bag punching him like a prizefighter.

"Where are we?"

"About ten miles outside Pinyon Forks," she whispered. Then Amber cocked her head. Now he heard the voices.

"Down here," said a male voice. The way he spoke made Carter think he was Anglo, Southern.

Who? he mouthed. She shrugged. Then she moved up close to his ear and whispered.

"I called your brother. He's coming. But the Subaru was leaking gas, and he told me to get you out."

And she had. How the devil had this little woman moved him?

Her lips brushed his ear as she spoke again. "I have their guns. Those guys. But someone else is here now."

"Jack?" he whispered.

"I don't think so."

From the top of the bank, seemingly right above them, came the voice again.

"Where is she?"

That one sounded Anglo, he thought.

Next came another voice, deeper, with a speaking pattern that lacked the Texas twang.

"They got away."

"They can't have gone far," came the reply.

Amber flattened into the warm earth beside him, covering her mouth with one hand and retrieving a gun from the waistband of her slacks. She looked like she knew what she was doing. She rolled to her side and then reached behind and beneath her blazer, laying a second gun on his chest. He took it, and their eyes met. He saw no fear now. Only a cold determination and willingness to do what was necessary. She would have made a good soldier. His gut twisted, so damn glad she had not been there with him in the Sandbox.

"They're right on our tails," said the first voice. "We have maybe another two minutes."

"But she's right here!" said his companion.

Amber's eyes widened. She was the only "she" out here.

"No time," repeated the first man. "Get my brother. We'll have to come back for her.

"Hurry up," said the first man.

A car door opened, the metal groaning a protest.

The same voice again. "Let's go."

Carter looked at Amber. Her hand was pressed to her mouth again as if to keep from screaming. Her eyes were wide. Seconds ticked by, and then two more doors slammed and tires patched out on the gravel that lined the shoulder of the road.

Amber slid her hand away from her mouth. "Are they gone?"

Carter nodded. "I think so."

"Should I check?" she asked.

He shook his head. There was no reason for her to see this. He could protect her from that image, the kind that stuck in your mind and flashed back like a thunderstorm.

They said they had two minutes.

"We wait," said Carter.

Insects buzzed in the grass above them, and the wind brushed through the long needles of the ponderosa pines on the opposite bank. Amber returned her gun to her waistband and then gripped his arm with two of hers as she huddled close.

"How did you get me out?" he asked.

"You walked, mostly."

"Mostly?"

There was a whooshing sound, as if from a strong gust of wind. Black smoke rose up behind them, billowing in a dark column in the bright blue sky.

"Fire," said Carter.

Had the men retrieved Muir and Leopold before setting the Subaru ablaze?

Tires crunched on sand. Amber's grip tightened, and she ducked her head.

"They're back," she whispered, her voice strained.

"Carter? Amber?"

He knew that voice. It was Jack.

"Here!" he yelled. When he stood, the dizziness came with him, clawing at him and making the ground heave. Amber was there beside him, steadying him, holding him so he didn't fall.

"Slow," she said. "Go slow."

She could have run to his brother. But she didn't. She helped him walk, leaning into him as she wrapped an arm about his middle and gripped his opposite arm, now draped over her narrow shoulders. Then he scrambled up the steep bank on his hands and knees toward the road topping the rise and saw the SUV consumed in flames.

Chapter Seven

Amber felt safe again, at least for now. Detective Bear Den had transported them back to Pinyon Forks and the Turquoise Canyon police station. On the way they had told Carter's brother everything. Once they arrived, she'd had a chance to wash her face and hands, brush out the powder from her hair and drink some water with Carter standing guard outside the door.

We'll have to come back for her.

Who where they? And why did they need to come back for her? She wrapped her arms about herself and shivered. She had gotten tangled up in something, but she didn't know what.

She now sat with Carter in Tribal Police Chief Tinnin's office devouring a sandwich, chips and a cookie provided by the same woman who prepared the meals for the prisoners. Amber was so hungry she barely tasted the food. Carter's was already gone, and he sat back to finish his third bottle of water.

Some of the powder had settled in his part, clinging to his black hair. He wore a new clean T-shirt courtesy of his brother who had a locker across the hall. He also wore an unbuttoned green-and-white chambray shirt that was obviously Jack's, because, though Carter was a big man, he had to roll the sleeves.

Carter watched her eat and smiled.

"Wish we had some fry bread," he said.

Fry bread! She hadn't had any since she'd visited her sister over the holidays. It was just one of many things she missed. She returned Carter's smile.

He lifted the water bottle and drank, his Adam's apple rising and falling with the rhythm of each swallow. Her mouth went dry, and her entire body electrified. Even after all this time he still made her want him without even trying.

She cut her gaze away, refusing to torture herself with the sight of him. But she was too weak, and her eyes found him again. The bottle lay between his two broad hands, tucked between strong thighs. She exhaled.

"Amber. You okay?"

She forced her gaze away from his groin, but it was too late. Now his eyes blazed in return, the sexual awareness crackling between them like static electricity.

"Amber," he whispered, leaning forward.

She shook her head but moved closer until his fingers brushed over her cheek, leaving heat blazing in their wake.

She wished they could go back in time, back to those two kids who had fallen in love, and try again. Tell her younger self to be wise and give Carter another chance. But it was too late now, because she could never ask him to leave their tribe, and she was too ashamed to stay.

Despite her reservations, her heart hammered in giddy excitement and her skin flushed.

Focus. You're in real trouble, and this man doesn't want a woman who walked away from her family.

Carter had loved her. But he loved his people and his place among them more. He was not leaving, and she was not staying. There was no future for them. Only more pain.

"Thank you for saving us back there," she said.

"I didn't get us out. I'd have been cuffed to the hand-grip in a smoldering wreck if not for you."

He'd been the reason they had a chance to get out of that SUV, and they both knew it.

Her smile drop away. "Did they find them?" she asked.

"No. Those other two got them out before torching the vehicle. No sign of them since."

"Oh, Carter. What's happening?"

He lifted his water. "I was hoping you'd know."

"I don't. I can't even imagine. It's like a nightmare."

Carter rubbed his neck. It was a gesture he used when unhappy, but she wondered now if it might stem from pain.

Carter had refused to go to the health clinic but had allowed Kurt to look him over. He declined the neck brace they recommended for the jolt he'd taken during the crash, but took the offered analgesic medication.

"Did you get through to your family?" asked Carter, changing the subject. Did he believe her? She couldn't tell.

"I did. Your brother let me use his desk phone. I called Kay. She'll get word to my mom and Ellie." But not her father. Her father had made it very clear that he wanted nothing to do with her ever again. Her stomach ached, and she felt even lower than before.

"Do you ever see them?" he asked. She could see the pain now, there in his tight expression and the watchful eyes. Did he still feel the ache that she carried like a stone in her heart?

"Sometimes. When I can. I see them at Kay's." Her younger sister had married at nineteen and moved to the smaller Rez communities of Koun'nde to the north of Pinyon Forks.

Now his eyes held accusation. "But you never came to see me again."

She hadn't. Not after that last time.

"Carter. I…" She thought of their last meeting. "I didn't think you'd want to see a *manzana*."

A *manzana* was Apache for an apple. It meant that she was red on the outside and white at the core.

She used the insult he'd thrown at her when he had been home recovering, and Yeager had still been listed as missing.

"I shouldn't have said that."

"You told me to go away, me and my *manzana* clothing." She lifted the hem of her ruined blazer to show that she still dressed like an Anglo working in an Anglo world.

His jaw tightened. And the glimmer of desire faded from his eyes, replaced with something hard and cold.

Detective Bear Den poked his head through the open doorway.

"The FBI is here. The real FBI."

"You find them—the guys that took us or the other two?" asked Carter.

"No." Jack shifted and rested a hand on his hip. "Vanished like ghosts." He inclined his head toward the door. "They have some questions."

Carter nodded and rose.

"Ah." Jack shifted again. "They want Amber first."

Carter hesitated, and she thought he might argue.

"You gonna sit in?" asked Carter.

Jack nodded and Carter resumed his seat. Amber stood, and her lunch rolled in her belly. She reminded herself that she had done nothing wrong. But it didn't quiet her nerves as she trailed behind Detective Bear Den.

She'd had a chance to clean up in the bathroom, but the fine powder still clung to the creases of her dark slacks and jacket, resisting her efforts to beat it away. And the smell of the gasoline and the air bags clung to her like skunk spray, making her head ache.

She felt as lost as the day she left her childhood home at seventeen, and just like on that day, she didn't know what would happen next.

Her world had somehow careened off-kilter, and all she wanted was to go to her crappy rented room in the guesthouse in Lilac, shower, sleep and wake up to find this entire day was just a nightmare.

Amber followed Detective Bear Den into the interrogation room where Tribal Police Chief Tinnin introduced her to two Anglos. Field Agent Parker rose and nodded. The man was in his thirties, cleanly shaven with extremely short hair that did nothing to hide his unfortunate ears that stuck out on each side of his head like pot handles. His partner, Field Agent Seager, had an under-bite that made his jaw thrust out. He also had blue eyes and prematurely gray hair. He stared at her as if he was hungry and she was lunch. Amber took a seat between Bear Den and Tinnin and the FBI across the table.

Over the next hour she was questioned and questioned again. She worked with an FBI artist to help create an image of the man she had seen at Mr. Ibsen's home and another for the driver.

It quickly became apparent that her miraculous escape from her offices at the copper mine and then again from the home of her supervisor had set off all kinds of alarms with the FBI. The line of their questions and the repetition gradually made it apparent that they were unconvinced that she was exceedingly lucky and that Carter's arrival was a timely coincidence.

"Ms. Kitcheyan? You were saying."

"Yes. I opposed the land exchange between the Lilac Mining Company and the US Forest Service. But it's not really up to me. Is it?"

The men exchanged a look.

"Are you a member of either WOLF or BEAR?"

"Of what?"

"Ms. Kitcheyan, did you have foreknowledge of today's attack?"

"No." She sounded shocked because that's how she felt. What was happening? She knit her brow and tried to think. She glanced to Detective Jack Bear Den who watched her with interest, and she suddenly felt all alone in the room. She glanced toward the door to the interrogation room, wondering where Carter might be.

"Did you take part in the planning of this attack?"

"No, I did not!" Did she sound defensive?

The three men stared at her as her throat began a familiar burn that told her tears were imminent.

"Why did those men take you from this station?"

"I don't know."

"But you did know them."

"No, I did not. They said they were FBI."

"Yes, that's what Chief Tinnin told us you said. But it seems more likely that you knew them."

"Well, I didn't."

"But you left the safety of the station. Why is that?"

"I wanted to smell the air."

Both men scowled at that.

"Let's go back to this morning," said Seager.

They started again, and when they got to the questions about her knowing the men who abducted her and Carter, she stopped them.

"I have helped you. But now you are just asking me the same thing over and over. So I'm not answering any more questions," she said. Now she sounded guilty as hell.

"That's certainly your right," said Parker, tugging at a pink ear. "But the man who murdered everyone in your office is still at large, and we thought you might want to help us with that."

"I do want to help you."

"We just want to be sure we understand. You left your office. You used the restroom. When you left the restroom you departed through the loading dock, breaking company procedure. There you saw the van with the driver, but you never heard a shot or saw the gunman."

"Again, yes."

"Are you sure you didn't, maybe, pass the shooter in the hallway?"

"I think I'd recall that."

The man's mouth quirked. "Do you?"

"Do I what?"

"Recall seeing the shooter?"

Chief Tinnin stood. "All right, gentlemen. You've had your interview. Detective Bear Den will walk you out. Two of my men will escort you off the tribe's land."

"We're not finished yet," said Parker.

"Oh, I'd disagree."

"We have to interview Carter Bear Den."

"Interview," said Tinnin. "Is that what you call this?"

Seager had the good manners to break eye contact. Parker just looked belligerent.

"It's federal land," said Seager.

"I'd disagree again. It is Apache land." He turned and motioned to the exit. Detective Bear Den held the door ahead of them.

Seager marched out.

Parker stopped and turned back to Tinnin before exiting. "US Marshals have been called. They're taking her into protective custody."

"She stays on tribal land," said Detective Bear Den.

His chief cast him a look of annoyance but did not oppose him before the federal agents.

Parker rubbed the bristle on his head and turned to Tinnin. "You blocking us from taking custody?"

"For now."

"There's already been two attempts on her life."

"Three," said Tinnin.

Parker stormed out after his partner.

Amber slumped in her chair, finally able to breathe again.

Chief Tinnin ambled to the door, pausing to glance back at Amber. "I can only stall them for so long.

Sooner or later they'll figure it out, and then they'll take you with them."

The door clicked shut, locking her in the interrogation room alone.

Chapter Eight

Carter waited while his brother walked the two FBI agents down the hall and out of sight. He supposed that meant they were not interviewing him next.

His brother's boss appeared after that.

"They don't want to take my statement?" asked Carter.

"They sure do. Nearly pissed themselves in anticipation. I called a halt, but they'll be back tomorrow. It's past suppertime and I have an agreement with the missus." Tinnin gave him a good hard look. "You have any idea what you've gotten yourself tangled up in?"

"I just know that Amber is in trouble."

Tinnin's gaze was unblinking. "You could say that." Tinnin looked at the tiled floor a moment and then lifted his gaze back to Carter. "You could also say that we have four suspects at large on our reservation, that your old girlfriend is the lone survivor in one hell of a mass slaying. That the van was recovered, but the gunman and his driver are still at large. That the man who admitted the gunman to the administration building in Lilac used the very same door as Amber and that the key card he used to gain admittance to the building came from a woman who worked in human resources until this morning when she was delayed by a bullet in her forehead. So, yes, son, I'd say Amber is in trouble."

"Why are they after her?" asked Carter.

"Don't know. But that random shooting doesn't seem random at all. Not when they took out her boss and then were here to greet Amber. Love to know how they knew where to find her. Love to know why she practically walked out there to meet them. You got any ideas about that one?"

"No, sir."

"Hmm." He pressed his free hand on his hip and shifted, resting a leg. "They called the US Marshals. I can stall but eventually she'll be transferred to the custody of them as a protected witness. They want you, too, but I can give you a choice."

"We could keep her here."

"Well, no. I don't have the manpower for protecting her. And I don't fancy a mass shooting at my police station, plus she's no longer one of your tribe."

Carter knew that Tinnin was also a Turquoise Guardian. He'd spent time in the sweat lodge with him and attended prayer circles.

"I was sent to Lilac to deliver a message to Amber from Kenshaw Little Falcon."

Tinnin slipped a hand in his front trouser pocket and thought on that a while.

"She's his sister's child, as I recall. You deliver it?"

"Not yet."

"Suppose you go in there and give it to her now."

"When the marshals come, I'm going with her."

"I'd advise against that."

Carter held his gaze.

"Why's that?"

"Might shorten your life expectancy."

Tinnin was an eagle catcher, and he was a strong man who had Carter's respect. He valued his opinion and wished like hell he could do as the older man suggested. Tinnin's insinuation that there was real danger only made Carter more determined to stay with Amber.

"I'll go see her now."

Tinnin's mouth turned down, and he nodded as if knowing already what Carter would do.

"She's not your responsibility, son. Not anymore."

Carter paused. He knew that in his head, but his heart whispered for him to protect her, that some part of her still belonged to him.

He headed to the interview room where he found Amber sitting with her arms folded on the table and her forehead resting on her arms.

"Amber?"

She popped up, looking dusty and tired and more beautiful than he had ever remembered. Her smile returned at the sight of him, and something in his middle squeezed. His throat went dry.

"Carter!" She looked relieved to see him. "Are you okay?"

"Ears are still ringing." He gave her a half smile. "How did it go in here?"

She threw herself back in her seat. "They think I know more than I do."

"What were you delivering to your boss?"

"They asked me that." She lifted her chin toward the closed door, referring to the FBI.

Carter waited and Amber met his gaze.

"Receiving slips." she said. "On a large delivery of

mining equipment. I log it in, and then Ibsen follows up with payment."

Carter wondered why someone would feel it necessary to kill everyone in the receiving department. Someone who hated open-pit mining would tend toward sabotaging the mining trucks or attacking mining equipment.

A knock sounded on the door. Amber stood and glanced at Carter. He had time to step between her and the door before it swung open.

Carter recognized Jack, and his shoulders dropped an inch.

"I called Ray and Dylan. We're taking you to a safe place for the night," said Jack.

"Where?"

"Ray suggested the lake."

He meant the restricted area of the reservation for members of the tribe only. It was where they often set a sweat lodge with the Turquoise Guardians. After purifying their bodies with sage smoke and steam, they would swim in the lake. There was only one way in, but the drive was over rough roads, and the journey would take an hour at least. More, now that it was dark. Still, he could think of no one he would rather have watching his back than Ray, Dylan and Jack.

They had joined the US Marines together and served their first tour in the same unit. More importantly, Carter had grown up with them and loved Ray and Dylan like brothers.

"They're en route. You two are heading out in a few minutes."

"You taking us?" asked Carter.

"Yes."

So it would be all four of them, Dylan, Ray, Carter and Jack—Tribal Thunder, as they were called among the Turquoise Guardians. All ex-military and some of the best fighters in the tribe. If anyone could keep Amber Kitcheyan safe, it was these men.

"Thank you."

Carter told Jack about the receiving slips and his suspicions. Jack leaned forward braced on stiff arms and fists balled on the surface of the desk, listening. When Carter finished, his brother gave them each a long look and said he needed to speak to the chief.

He walked them to the squad room and left Carter and Amber by his desk.

"Wait here."

Jack joined Chief Tinnin in his office.

Amber's attention wandered over Jack's workstation, catching on the photos. She smiled, lifting the frame that held the photo of his marine buddies. She knew them all, of course, would have graduated with them had she not left. Jack and Carter stood with arms locked around each other's shoulders in the Sandbox with their best friends and fellow tribe members Ray Strong, Hatch Yeager and Dylan Tehauno. Amber said nothing, just pointed Carter out with an elegant index finger and smiled. Carter tried and failed to avoid glancing at Hatch. He cleared his throat, trying to force back the punch of grief. How could Jack even bear to look at it?

Amber replaced the frame to the desk and lifted the one in the metal frame, looking at a photo of his family. Carter felt the tension in his chest ease. His breathing returned to normal, but sweat still popped out on his brow.

"Is that Tommy?"

Carter stepped closer, wiping away the sheen of sweat, hoping she wouldn't notice.

"Yeah. His graduation. That's eight years ago now."

When Amber had last seen him, his younger brother had been a scrawny freshman who was tall but so thin a stiff breeze could blow him down.

"He got big."

"Even bigger now," said Carter.

She glanced toward the office where his twin was deeply engaged in conversation with the chief.

"But not as big as Jack."

Carter laughed. "No one is that big."

She returned her focus to the photo in her hands. "What's Tommy doing now?"

"Shadow Wolf," said Carter, his chest lifting at the thought that his little brother had joined the elite Native American—only branch of Immigration and Customs Enforcement.

"Wow. Working on the border tracking bad guys?"

Carter nodded, his smile full of pride.

"That's right. Traffickers mostly."

"I thought he wanted to join the military like his big brothers."

Carter's smile dropped. "I talked him out of it."

"Hmm." Amber's attention went back to the photo. "And Kurt. He pilots the air ambulance?"

"He's also a paramedic and a Hot Shot."

"Your mom looks exactly the same. And your father? How's he doing?"

"He's good. Still ranching." Carter watched her and saw her brow knit.

"He really is big, isn't he?" Her index finger fell on Jack's image.

Carter returned his attention to the photograph.

All his brothers had long hair back then. He still did, and so did Tommy. This photo showed why Jack kept his hair short. Three brothers with long, straight black hair and Jack, his hair soft brown and showing a definite wave. His gray eyes startling next to the deep brown of the rest of the brothers.

"He ate more than us," said Carter, using a family joke that didn't seem very funny just now.

"Jack doesn't look like you three."

Carter locked his jaw and made a sound that was noncommittal.

"Not just his hair, but his body type, too."

It was true.

"I always noticed it, but this photo… Wow," she said.

Amber replaced the frame to the exact place it had been on Jack's desk.

Carter wrestled with a decision and acted on impulse.

"Amber. I'd like to tell you something. But it's private."

She turned her dark eyes on him, and his gut twisted as the need roused inside him, causing his blood to race.

"I understand."

"I don't want you speaking to anyone about it, not even Jack. Especially not Jack."

"Does it have to do with the case?"

"No. It's personal."

"Then I agree."

She was cautious. He liked that. Thoughtful and observant and smart.

"My brother, he…he doesn't believe that we have the same father."

Her dark brows arched, forming an elegant curve, and her lips pursed. But she didn't seem shocked or scandalized. Of course this wasn't her mother they were talking about. It was his. His mother who taught special education for twenty-eight years at one of the tribe's elementary schools, and he was implying that she had been unfaithful to their dad. It made his stomach ache.

"I'd have to agree. He doesn't look Apache. At least not only Apache."

Carter felt a stab of grief in his heart. It was a suspicion that he had tried to allay for years.

"Parents aren't perfect," she said. "They make mistakes."

The way she said this made him wonder if she spoke from personal experience.

"You mean your parents?" he asked.

She rubbed the scar above her mouth as she met his gaze. The corners of her mouth dipped, and she turned to the windows as three vehicles pulled in before the station, their headlights flashing bright in the fading daylight.

She pointed at the vehicles. "Is that Ray and Dylan?"

She was avoiding the question.

He didn't let go. "Amber, what did they say to you to make you surrender your membership in this tribe?"

Her scowl deepened. "That was a long time ago."

"Not so long."

She turned from the window and laid the palm of her hand on his chest. His breathing caught.

"Why don't we talk about that another time?"

He wanted to press, but more than that, he wanted to press Amber against him.

Carter slipped his hands in his front pockets, and his fingers touched the folded paper.

He drew out the sealed white envelope he had been charged with delivering.

"This is for you."

She stared at the offering. "Is that the letter from my uncle?"

He nodded, extending his arm across the gap between them. She hesitated and then accepted the letter. Her fingers brushed over the top of his index finger. The tingling charge of electricity fired up his arm, sending his skin to gooseflesh. Their eyes met and held. Did she feel it, too?

Her breath caught and her mouth opened. His gaze fixed on that appealing pink mouth as her teeth clamped on her lower lip.

Carter released the envelope and stepped back, his skin flushed and his heart pounding. Whatever had been between them, it wasn't over. That much he knew.

Amber stared at the message. If not for that small white rectangle of paper, she'd be dead right now.

Amber's hands trembled as she tore the end of the envelope and removed the folded white sheet of paper, opened it and stared. Then she glanced up at Carter.

"I don't understand," she said.

"What does it say?"

Amber turned the paper so he could see the blank page.

"What does it mean?" asked Amber.

But Carter was afraid he understood. Kenshaw Little

Falcon had known what was coming at the Lilac Copper Mine, and he wanted his sister's child protected.

"I have to see Jack and I need to speak to your uncle."

"You don't think…" Her words trailed away as she must have reached the same conclusion as Carter. "No. That can't be."

He did not offer reassurances.

Carter had the strong urge to drop the paper in the garbage can. Instead he brought Amber into the chief's office and shared the letter with them. Jack's breath came in a long audible exhalation of air.

"I'll go see him tonight. He must have known what we'd make of this."

"It doesn't prove anything," said Amber.

"It's not good," said Jack to the page.

The chief slipped on a glove and dropped the envelope and blank page in an evidence bag.

Chapter Nine

Carter and Amber were gathered up in an impromptu caravan. Before them rode Dylan in a white pickup truck, the man who'd earned the most honors in the service. He was always where he was supposed to be and a born leader. It was natural for him to take point.

Next came Jack's truck carrying Carter in the front passenger seat and Amber on the smaller seat behind them. Ray took the tail, watching their back as always. Ray had a well-earned reputation for causing trouble and making decisions that were questionable at best. He had served time for some of his life choices, but he was rock solid when it came to Tribal Thunder. They trusted him, and she believed that he had never let them down.

Carter glanced back at Amber, silhouetted by the lights of Ray's truck.

"You okay?" he asked.

She nodded, but she wasn't. Amber had reached the point well past exhaustion back at the station, and she was not sure how she even remained upright.

"You can stretch out on the backseat. It will take a while to get there," he said. Though, how she would sleep when they bumped and jolted over the unpaved road he wasn't sure.

"Actually," said Jack, "we're not going to the lake."

Carter frowned at the change in plan. "Why not?"

"We didn't want Tinnin to know where you are. Then he doesn't have to lie."

"The lake is a very defensible position," said Carter, his mind slipping back to his military training.

"But they don't have fry bread or a barbecue grill out there."

"So you picked food over position?"

"No, our mom is picking food over position. She found out you are back from Lilac, and no amount of talk will convince her you are all right until she sees you with her own eyes."

"Does she know about Amber?"

"Of course. You think she'd cook fry bread on a Tuesday night for us?"

"Did you tell her it was dangerous?" asked Carter.

"Yes and she threatened to have Aunt Gigi drive her out to the lake with the grill and a vat of oil in the back of the truck."

Carter accepted defeat.

Jack spoke over the seat to Amber. "We're going to your sister's."

Carter saw the smile lift her tired face.

"Your mom will be there."

Her smile dropped like a curtain. Amber groaned and sank back in her seat.

"Bad idea," said Carter.

Jack laughed. "Then you tell her." He offered his phone.

Carter relented but crossed his arms in frustration.

"Relax. I called in some favors. Nobody gets past our police unless they recognized them."

Carter lifted a brow, knowing there was no department overtime. "What did you promise them?"

"Mom's fry bread."

That would do it.

"And I'm starving," said Jack.

They arrived twenty minutes later to hugs and tears by both moms. Amber's mom, Natalie, hugged Carter. The familiar odor of whiskey and cigarette smoke clung to her, but she didn't seem so drunk that she was slurring her words. Amber's sister Kay showed them in, and Carter and Jack were seated as the guests of honor. Ray and Dylan joined Carter's aunt Gigi and uncle Paul at the table. Their father, Delane, was in the backyard with Kay's husband, Aiden, cooking steaks. Kay's children, both under two, were already in bed, but Amber and Kay crept down the hall to see them.

Amber followed Kay, but her sister stopped shy of the bedroom door and turned in the hall.

"Are you all right?" asked Kay.

"Just exhausted."

"I can't believe he has the nerve to come here after what he said to you," said Kay. Amber had told Kay exactly what Carter had called her, and Kay seemed disinclined to forget.

"His only other choice was to roll out of a moving truck."

Kay sniffed. "He still has no idea. Does he?"

Amber sighed, hoping someday Carter would listen.

"I can't believe what happened today. Those Anglos are crazy. When I think what might have happened." Kay hugged her again. Then quickly let her go and smoothed Amber's blazer. "This is filthy. You need clothes."

"I do."

Kay swiped at her tearing eyes, and her lower lip protruded in a gesture that Amber knew forecast more tears.

"Don't. I'm here now. It will be all right." Except the Feds wanted her in custody as a witness or possibly a suspect and Tinnin had warned that the tribe couldn't protect her for long. Her stomach roiled, the acid sloshing like water in the washer. Amber changed the subject. "How's Dad?" Amber's chest hurt as she waited. Kay's eyes lifted to the ceiling before returning to meet hers.

Kay picked at her cuticle, tearing away a bit of skin. "You know. The same."

The same was bad. That meant too much booze and too much gambling. Amber recalled the last time she had seen her dad.

You are my children. I made you and I can make more just like you.

"It's stealing," she had said. "You're a thief."

His face had turned purple as he ordered her out of his house.

Kay's words broke into her musings.

"They lost the truck and horses. They don't have anything left, really. Just the house, but you know, it belongs to HUD. And Dad got arrested."

"Arrested?"

"Yeah. For writing bad checks. He's got a court date. But… Amber, I think he'll have to serve some time."

She didn't know how she felt about that. Was it long overdue or just another link in a chain of sorrow?

At least Kay and Ellie had roofs over their heads, and her sisters were free and clear of debt. That made her feel some sense of accomplishment.

"And Mom?" asked Amber, recalling trying to convince their mother to leave, too. All of them. Her mother hadn't wanted to admit there was a problem, so she had watched Amber go. According to her mom, Amber was just on some kind of extended journey to find herself, as if her father had not done a thing wrong.

"She needs some help sometimes."

Amber stiffened. "You are not giving her money."

Kay shrugged. "Food mostly. Safer that way."

Amber's lips seemed fused. It must have been hard for Kay being here, especially when her husband, Aiden, had a good job in the tribe's highway department.

Silence yawned between them.

"I'm sorry this is all on you now," said Amber.

"And I'm sorry you had to leave. You know, if you just tell them what happened, maybe…"

"I'm not going to embarrass them. He is still my father."

Kay stared at the worn carpet runner and nodded. Then she reached for the door, and they crept into the room to admire the two sleeping boys.

When they returned from the bedrooms, Amber wore one of Kay's pretty cotton dresses in a rich coral color with a wide yoke and belt. She'd also cast off her flats for silver sandals. Amber wished she'd had time to shower.

Carter had been in conversation with Dylan, but his gaze locked on her and then dropped as his eyes swept over her. His smile was full of appreciation, and Amber felt her cheeks heat.

"That dress never looked so good," whispered Kay and left her to help Aunt Gigi set the table.

Amber's brother-in-law, Aiden, held the kitchen door open as Carter's uncle Paul and Carter's dad stepped into the kitchen, bringing with them the aroma of charred steak. Amber, Kay and their mom laid the rest of the meal upon the table as Carter's mother, Annette, forked the last of the fry bread from the bubbling pot of hot oil. Everyone dug in. The fry bread was so hot, the transfer from platter to plate had to be done with speed and dexterity. Carter had not expected to be so famished, but he ate with a good appetite. Amber ate more than he had ever seen her as her mother jabbered on about Ellie, who was away at college. Amber was happy for her youngest sister's achievements, but there was a pang of regret at never having seen the inside of a college classroom.

Her mother never mentioned her dad, and Amber did not ask about him.

Carter watched the stiffness between Amber and her mother with curiosity. He knew there was bad blood but did not know exactly what caused Amber to leave home while he was away on his first tour in the Sandbox. But he had an idea it was tied to the reason she'd given him back his ring. Now he found he wanted to fill in those blank spots.

Finally the dishes were cleared. Amber rubbed her eyes and stifled a series of yawns.

"Are we staying the night?" asked Carter, suddenly so weary he feared he wouldn't be able to stand.

Dylan answered, "My place. It's here in Koun'nde. I

have two bedrooms. Ray, Jack and I will take watch, and Jack recruited some of the tribal police for surveillance."

Carter did not wait but rose to his feet and helped Amber stand. Carter's mom forced the remains of the fry bread on Ray and the uneaten dessert on Dylan. Kay gave Amber a travel bag, which he assumed held clothing and such.

Amber was asleep on his shoulder before they had left the drive. They passed two tribal vehicles on the way, which was reassuring.

When they reached their destination, Carter waited in the truck with Jack as Ray and Dylan swept the perimeter. When they returned, Carter woke Amber, who was so groggy he had to walk her up the steps.

Her scent and her warm body stirred him. She felt so right there against him, and it made him long for all that they had missed. Their host directed him. Carter was pleased but not surprised to see that Dylan's house, like his person, was neat, clean and welcoming. The guest room for Amber was functional, with a queen-size bed and side table, but looked more like a library with all the bookshelves stacked to overflowing and a sagging overstuffed reading chair beside a floor lamp.

Ray and Dylan stopped in the hall as Carter assisted Amber in, where she sank into the comfortable chair.

Ray peered around the room. "Geesh, Dylan, you actually read all these?"

"Not yet."

"Looks like a library."

"There aren't a lot of books up here."

"There are now," said Ray.

Dylan had laid a clean towel on the bed with a bag from the drugstore.

"Got you two some things. There's a toothbrush, comb and some travel-sized things in there," he said and blushed. Then he thumbed over his shoulder. "You're in my room. Clean towel. You can use my shaving kit. Take any clothing you like."

Amber thanked Ray and Dylan, who left them alone. Amber left the chair to explore Dylan's offerings, lifting the bag and passing Carter one of two new toothbrushes.

"This was sweet of Dylan," she said, her voice slurred from exhaustion.

"Razor?" she asked.

He nodded his head. "Sure."

She handed over the razor and then leaned forward and rubbed the coarse whiskers on his jaw with her palm. He struggled not to capture her hand against his cheek; it felt so damned right.

A tired smile curled her lips. "Rough."

He was dead on his feet, nearly swaying with fatigue, yet that simple touch had electrified him as if he'd stuck his finger in a light socket.

"That dress is very pretty on you."

"Kay made it. She's great at sewing."

It wasn't the sewing but the fit that was perfect, showing Amber's curves and just enough leg.

His attention flicked from her hand to her eyes. She watched him, her dark eyes hooded. He tried to remember why he shouldn't kiss her. Remember the reason it was a bad idea. They were now tied inexorably to the worst murder spree to take place in Arizona. And she was, at best, a witness and, at worst, a suspect. But that wasn't the only reason, not all of it anyway. There was the ring. The one she'd dropped in the dirt and he still had.

And yet, she captivated him. No, disturbed, that was a better word. Yes, she disturbed him. Deep down and relentlessly.

She let her fingers drag over his jaw and down his throat. He captured her hand in both of his and pressed her palm over his heart, pinning her before him as he debated his choices, let her rest or...

Amber cast him a certain look.

Decision made.

Chapter Ten

Amber didn't look away or retreat as Carter stepped closer. Instead she lifted her hand to finger the collar of his shirt, letting the back of her hand graze his neck. In her wake his skin buzzed and tingled, every nerve alive and yearning for her touch. Carter lifted his hand to cup the back of her head, and she tipped forward, lifting to her toes.

"Bad idea," he said.

"The worst," she replied.

Then she tilted her head and kissed him. Her soft full lips set off a tremor inside him. The epicenter lay south of his belt. He planted a hand at the center of her back and pulled, thrusting her forward. She fell against his chest. Her hands splayed over his shoulders and then slid up until they threaded in his hair. She seemed starved for him, and he felt like the desert in a long-awaited rain.

Her mouth opened, and her tongue darted into his mouth. Carter tipped her across one arm to give him better access to her mouth and neck and…he opened one eye to find a place where he could stretch her out. What he saw was Dylan's desk piled with books.

Carter groaned and drew her back to her feet. Then

he broke the kiss and stepped away, keeping only one hand on her arm to be sure she was steady on her feet, then letting her go.

He's seen that expression before. That sort of dazed stare and crooked smile of pleasure.

"Why, Amber? Why now?" he asked.

She flushed. "I just thought… I hoped that it wasn't as good as I remembered."

"And?" he asked, then tensed waiting for her reply.

"Better. So much better," she whispered and gripped both her hands before her as if to make them behave.

"Yeah," he said and rubbed his neck. "What are we going to do about it?"

"I don't know." She glanced toward the door. "They're taking me. Maybe soon. Tinnin said so."

It added urgency to his need. The thought of losing her again hit him hard. He fought it and almost told her he wouldn't let them take her. But it was a lie. She'd know there was no way to keep her from federal custody other than running, maybe to Mexico. And then he'd lose it all, his medicine society, his friends, his family and his tribe. The thought washed him cold, and he took a step back.

Her smile was weary, as if belonging to a much older woman, one who knew the disappointments life can bring.

"We should get some sleep."

"Yes. We should."

He wanted to tell her that he still had feelings for her and that he'd never gotten past the hurt and betrayal of her leaving.

Instead he played it safe, not willing to risk her rejection again because, oh, how it hurt the last time.

Still hurt like a phantom limb, gone but still aching, the nerves confused at losing something so vital.

"It was nice to see everyone together tonight," she said.

Did she miss her family as much as he missed her? He couldn't imagine it, being away from them and his home. Every tour of duty he served was endurable only because he knew he would one day come home.

"Yeah."

"Dylan looks good. But Ray seems a little sad, still."

Yeager had been his best friend, Carter knew. Amber knew that, as well.

He felt like the cacti, down there on the flat scorched earth far below the mountains just waiting for the rain. Only he had waited nine years for Amber to come back, to explain, to apologize for turning her back on him and their future together. But she never came. She was here now only because she had no other choice. It hurt knowing that.

She fidgeted with a button on the dress Kay had made.

"I'm glad to see Ray doing well. A Hot Shot, too, Kay says. She was surprised after his troubles."

Was she referring to the depression or the drinking or the car he flipped while his blood alcohol level was twice the legal limit?

"He's doing okay now."

"Do you guys ever talk about it?"

He met her cautious stare and considered kissing her in an effort to get her to stop talking, but he was too slow.

"Yeager, I mean."

He locked his jaw.

"What happened to him, Carter?"

CARTER TENSED AT Amber's question about his fallen comrade, Hatch Yeager. She leaned away to look up at him, and he grimaced at the gut-twisting reaction that always punched him low and deep when he thought of Hatch.

His face flushed as he recalled the last time Amber had asked that question. He was nineteen and home after two weeks in a field hospital in Baghdad, followed by eighteen days of rehab stateside. After they'd finished picking all the tiny metal fragments from his right arm and shoulder, they'd left him to pick at all the tiny emotional fragments of the attack. Carter had breathed in grief like air and needed psychological help. She'd visited him then, in that dark time.

They only knew Hatch was missing then. Abandoned, was there any worse fate? He looked down at Amber and some tiny bridge formed in his mind. Had she abandoned him or had he abandoned her?

Amber waited. He hedged, still trying to avoid speaking of this.

"Maybe now isn't the best time," he said. "I should let you rest."

He watched the hopeful expression crumble to disappointment.

"I mean, especially not after today." He left the rest unspoken. Not on the day when her coworkers had been murdered.

She met his gaze. "Especially today. Carter, every time I rest I think of them. Every time I close my eyes I see Nancy smiling at her desk or Frank or Trisha. And I feel so guilty that I wasn't there and so grateful, too."

Carter straightened. She understood.

"But it wasn't your fault," he said.

"Wasn't it? If what the FBI said is true, then I brought that to them because of the error I pointed out to my boss. I did that."

"But you didn't know."

Her eyes narrowed, and her lips pressed tight. "And whatever happened to Hatch wasn't your fault either, even if you feel it was."

He tore his gaze from hers. She rested a hand on his back.

"Tell me, Carter. Please."

"Okay."

It wasn't okay, of course. Never would be.

"I heard he was found," she said.

"Identified," corrected Carter. "The Marines notified his family in July of '09. We got him back in August and buried him with full honors."

His body. A casket. A flag.

"I'm so sorry."

"Yeah. It's been hard." Because they were always together, a team. The Bear Den twins, Ray, Dylan and Hatch...and Hatch. Carter's throat closed, and so he clenched his teeth, fighting for control.

Amber began a rhythmic stroking of his back. Her small hand was warm and soothing.

She was brave to tread this ground again after what he had said the last time she asked. It showed she was willing to give him a second chance. Was he willing to do the same?

On her last visit he'd been angry at Amber and himself, and so he had barked at her like a rabid dog.

"Go away, Amber. It's what you always wanted, to be rid of this place. So go."

"I just wanted—"

"Look at you. All dressed up like an Anglo." He had swept her with a look of contempt. *"You're a man-zana."*

The tears had come then, and she'd turned away, dashing down the steps and out of his life.

"That's right. Run away. It's all you're good at."

Amber's hand stopped, and he opened his eyes, looking down at her lovely face. She deserved better than him.

"Is it better to pretend he does not still live in the hearts of all four of you?"

She was asking what to do—remember them? Try to forget. And she was right. Yeager wasn't dead. He was the ghost that sat among them. He thought of the tattoo he had chosen with the help of their shaman and head of their medicine society. Five feathers. One for each direction and one for the center of their circle—Yeager.

She moved to sit on the bed, folding up her legs and retrieving a pillow, which she hugged before her, chin resting on the top. He sat beside her, his feet on the floor.

He would answer her question, and the realization exhausted him before he even spoke a single word.

He started talking. "Twenty-two hundred hours. May 1. We're setting up an observation post in the death triangle. It's a spot near Al-Yusufiyah, in Iraq, a bad spot. Our first tour. We were so charged to see action." He shook his head in disgust at his naïveté. "So our SFC says he wants Bear Den and Tehauno in the first Humvee with him. We all know he means me, but Jack just winks at me and takes off for the first Humvee, and the SFC doesn't make a big deal of the joke, just lets Jack go." Now, Jack felt as if Carter's wounds

were his fault, but Carter kept that to himself. "So because of Jack, SFC Mullins hesitates before choosing
the third man, and Ray yells, 'And Strong.' Mullins,
our sergeant says, 'Fine, Strong.' But you can hear he
isn't thrilled, and we all know he likes Yeager better
than Ray because Ray is a wiseass." But not anymore.
Not since that night. Carter swallowed.

Amber placed her hand on his shoulder, silently encouraging him to go on.

"That leaves second in command, Sergeant Tromgartner, with me, Yeager and our interpreter, Ahmed,
in the second Humvee. I'm annoyed with Jack because
he's got Mullins. I'm stuck with Tromgartner who always drives, and I can drive if I'm with Mullins, so I tell
Yeager to take the backseat." Such a small decision but
one to change all their lives. "We roll south of Baghdad
and set up the observation post with the two Humvees
one hundred and fifty yards apart. facing opposite directions, trying to keep insurgents from attacking our
guys on the road. Instead we're ambushed by a group
with automatic weapons and explosives."

Amber set aside the pillow and took his hands. He
hadn't realized he had been pounding a fist against his
knee until she held him still. He glanced at her, and she
nodded for him to continue.

"They blew us to hell. That second Humvee. We
were on fire, and my sergeant was bleeding."

"That's how you injured your arm?"

He glanced at the spiderweb of white scars. "Yeah.
Parts of the Humvee and the IEDs. Because of the
smoke, I couldn't see Yeager or Ahmed. They were just
gone. Tossed from the vehicle. So I grabbed Tromgartner
and ran him to the first Humvee. They shot Tromgart-

ner as I'm running him back. Then I look back and see Ahmed running after us. I yell 'Where's Hatch?' He points down the hill, and I see the insurgents already at the second Humvee. I drop Tromgartner, and Ray and Dylan have him. I turn back for Yeager, but Jack stops me. He muscles me into the Humvee and we take off."

"You thought they killed him," whispered Amber.

"No. I *prayed* they killed him. I prayed for that every minute of every day. But they didn't." They'd tortured him for months. They'd tortured him. All because Carter had taken the front seat. Or chosen to rescue his sergeant instead of searching for his friend.

"They buried him here," said Amber. "I've visited his grave."

Amber's fingers trailed over the white puckered skin that crisscrossed over his right forearm. The tattoo on his upper arm and shoulder covered some of the damage there.

"How badly were you injured?" she asked, tracing the white scars.

He removed the chambray shirt, showing her the rest, peeling back the sleeve of his borrowed T-shirt so it ringed his shoulder.

Amber winced at the damage. But her fingers continued to dance over his skin like a blind woman reading braille.

"Would you blame him if the reverse had happened?" she asked.

"I don't know. I might."

She didn't tell him that Hatch Yeager was now at peace or that it wasn't his fault or that these things happen in war or any of the other things that people say. Instead she said the one thing no one else had thought to say.

"I'm sorry. I'm sorry for you and for Hatch. He was a wonderful friend to all of you. I know you miss him."

And when he needed Carter, he had not been there. Carter felt his throat tighten, but he held on.

"I'm sorry about your friends, too."

She gave him a tight little smile and swallowed before speaking again.

"This is new," she said stroking the skin of his upper arm and the artwork depicting a medicine shield with five dangling feathers, one for each of them, Dylan, Ray, Carter, Jack and Yeager. Each feather was adorned with a turquoise bead like the one given to them as baby boys at their birth. The stretched hide of the shield depicted the imprint of a bear paw.

"I've had it since I came back. We all have one."

"The same one?"

"No, your uncle, Kenshaw Little Falcon, helped each of us choose the design." He could say no more because being chosen as a warrior of Tribal Thunder, though a great honor, was as much a secret as was the rituals of his medicine society, the Turquoise Guardians. He could not share this business, especially with a woman.

"A bear for a Bear Den. Is Jack's shield also the track of a bear?"

Carter frowned because he did not understand his shaman's choice of symbol or placement. He and Ray and Dylan were all told to choose a medicine shield, and their spiritual leader had selected their talisman. An eagle for Ray to help him see more clearly and make better decisions. The track of a bobcat for Dylan to help him see what is hidden. But Jack was told to depict a medicine wheel on his back to help him know which direction to go.

"Jack's is a medicine wheel," said Carter.

"Good choice."

But different than the rest of them. Yet another visible separation between them.

"I do not think he likes it."

"No?"

Carter was uncomfortable speaking of his brother's insecurities.

"He told me that he wanted an animal spirit. Ray Strong doesn't have a track. His is an eagle to help him see farther ahead. But mine is a bear track and Dylan has the track of a bobcat for stealth. Jack doesn't have an animal totem."

"A medicine wheel is a powerful symbol."

"It makes him feel different. He wanted a shield, like the rest of us."

"But he's not like the rest of you."

Carter stiffened and drew his arm from her grip. "He's my brother."

Amber dropped her gaze and nodded. "They are all your brothers—Tommy, Kurt, Jack, Dylan, Ray and Hatch."

She gave him an open look, and he wondered if he might have a second chance with her.

But first he needed to know why she had gone.

"I want to know what happened."

"When?"

"The day you left us."

"I tried to tell you."

"I remember. You were worked up about your father's truck."

"No. It wasn't about his truck. It was about you treating me as a child, instead of your future wife. You actually called me childish."

"We were seventeen. We were both childish, Amber."

"Maybe. But you worked everything out with my dad. You didn't even include me until after you gave him your signing bonus."

"It's only money."

"Not to my father. To him it's a disease."

"I solved the problem."

"You made it worse."

"Oh, come on. Can't be that bad. Certainly not bad enough for you to rescind your membership in the tribe."

Amber slipped from the bed. Slowly she drew to her feet and motioned to the door.

"I think you better go."

Chapter Eleven

Carter went out to the living room to find both Ray and Dylan in conversation. Ray had a pistol in a shoulder harness beneath his left arm and Dylan's rifle with a scope leaned against the kitchen table. Just seeing his friends there made him feel better. This was what it meant to have brothers of choice, if not of blood. He couldn't ask for better fighters or better men.

He told them about the message he had delivered, and Ray and Dylan agreed to go visit Kenshaw Little Falcon and ask him about the blank page. He thanked them formally in Apache and spent a few minutes catching them up on all that had happened during the day.

They hadn't even asked. He needed help, and that was all they had to know. They trusted him, and he trusted them with his life.

A thought struck him. They hadn't asked. If he said it was important, then it was important. If he said it was life or death, then it was just that.

But when Amber told him he was not to pay her father's debts, he had downplayed her concerns. He hadn't listened, and he hadn't trusted her. She was trying to protect her sisters and her parents. She was try-ing to respect her father and keep him from jail and guard her sister's future. She'd spent a decade alone, without her people.

"You two back together?" asked Jack.

Carter groaned. It didn't take long to spill his guts. Amber opened the door to her room, cast them a ferocious glare and headed to the bathroom.

Carter felt gut shot.

"You okay, man?" asked Ray. Ray would understand mistakes if anyone would. One had landed him in jail for over a year and another had cost him his best friend's life. Or that was how he saw it, and nothing he or Dylan said could change his mind.

Perceptions. Reality. Was there really a difference?

He glanced to the hall where Amber exited the bathroom, freshly showered, her wet hair leaving a stain on the back of the short sleeveless nightie that must have been Kay's. She glanced at him, scowled and then shut the bedroom door with a little too much force.

"I screwed up again," said Carter.

Ray punched his arm, redirecting his attention. "Look on the bright side. Tomorrow you get another chance to screw things up all over again."

Dylan glanced at his watch. "Already tomorrow."

"I should talk to her," he said.

"Let her rest. Want a beer?" asked Ray.

"Naw. I'm beat. I'm going to hit the sack."

His friends exchanged a look.

"What?" he asked.

"Should I set up a perimeter around Amber's room?" asked Dylan.

Carter made a face and stalked toward the bathroom. It didn't hit him until he was in the shower how bone-weary he really was. He made it to Ray's bedroom, dropped the towel and slipped into bed. Amber's sister had given her an overnight bag as if she were preparing to flee the country. Maybe she was. But the next time she agreed to speak to him, he was going to give her the respect of listening without assuming the worst. He was downright ashamed of himself for doing that before and worse still, for not even recognizing what he had done. Was that why she left? Because he would not listen or understand?

Carter tossed, punched the pillow and finally eased into a restless sleep. He woke often to stare at the glowing red numbers on Ray's bedside clock before finally waking with a start at the gentle rapping on his door. He was shocked to see that the gentle gray light of morning found him still asleep.

"Bro?" That was Jack. He sagged, knowing he was hoping it had been Amber.

"Yeah," he called.

The door creaked open, and Jack's face appeared in the gap.

"Chief Tinnin is on the phone. He says he's got an FBI agent in his office, and one of the two new Feds is Black Mountain Apache." Jack cast Carter one last look. "We have to go in."

AN HOUR LATER Carter and Amber reported to the tribal police station. Amber had been cool and polite this morning. The walls were definitely back in place, and he knew he had been the mason.

At the station, they were introduced to FBI Field Agent Luke Forrest. Jack had told them en route that Forrest was instrumental in busting the crystal meth labs operating on the White Mountain Apache Reservation, but Carter saw another *manzana*. Had to be, because a man working for the FBI could be nothing else.

Carter took Amber's elbow as they entered the squad room, intending to keep her close, but felt her body tense at his touch. Carter sized up Field Agent Luke Forrest. The man's suit fit perfectly, revealing a slim, athletic white lawman with the head of an Apache. He wore his hair short in a military style Carter himself had once favored. But not anymore. He was never going to hide who and what he was at the core.

Chief Tinnin made introductions. Carter regarded Agent Forrest. The FBI had wisely sent the only Apache agent they had to negotiate the transfer of Amber to the US Marshals' protection.

Forrest cast them a confident smile that matched his handshake. His eyes were dark and cold as flint. He nodded to Amber, but his gaze lingered—whether out of appreciation or desire to take her from Turquoise Canyon, Carter wasn't sure. Carter had to hand it to Forrest. The warmth of his smile never wavered.

Carter kept Amber slightly behind him, but Agent Forrest spoke to her first and in English.

As a full-blood Mountain Apache, Forrest had the same genetic roots, but his people and Carter's had been enemies in the Apache Wars. Some things are never forgotten. The Turquoise Canyon Apache were of the Tonto Apache. Not Mountain Apache. Tonto was a name Carter despised because it was given to them by the Spanish and meant either crazy or moron, depending on who you asked. The Tonto Apache's language was different enough that most other Apache tribes could not understand them. They called themselves Dilzhę'é, but neither their Athabaskan neighbors of Black Mountain nor the US government paid any attention to what they called themselves. Carter shook his head in disgust at the thought of who the US government had sent in as their first choice.

"Ms. Kitcheyan," said Forrest, "Chief Tinnin has told me that you know why I'm here. You are an important witness to the mass slayings in Lilac and, as I understand it, may be able to identify our killer."

Amber nodded.

"Then both you and Mr. Bear Den are key witnesses."

"Don't you have to catch someone before you need witnesses?" asked Jack, placing a hand on his hip to reveal his gold tribal police detective's shield and the pistol holstered at his hip. Carter had questioned Jack's choice to join the tribal police as many of their people saw them as little better than the Arizona highway patrol, working for the establishment instead of the people. But right now, Carter felt lucky.

Forrest kept right on talking as if Detective Bear Den were background noise.

"I know you feel an obligation to see this man and his accomplice brought to justice. I know you lost many friends and colleagues yesterday."

AMBER LACED HER hands before her, but she said nothing. Her stomach churned.

"The attack and the subsequent attempts on your life, one right here on your tribal lands, make it clear to us that you both need protection."

"But I don't want protection," said Amber. "I want to go home."

Even as she said it, she knew her request sounded

crazy. She stared at the four men. Tribal Police Chief Wallace Tinnin, Carter Bear Den, Detective Jack Bear Den and FBI Agent Forrest. Her skin went damp as she imagined being caged in a safe house. Trapped with a man she'd once loved before she discovered that he did not trust her. Back then she believed love and trust were one and the same. But they were not, and she could not live without both.

"What if I refuse?" she asked.

Agent Forrest and Chief Tinnin exchanged a look. Agent Forrest got the short stick and faced her with hands open. A trick she used herself to put people at ease. It was a gesture that was intended to speak to the primal brain. *See? I have no weapons.*

"Ms. Kitcheyan, like it or not, you are a federal witness. You arrived only moments after the shooting at the home of Harvey Ibsen. Later you were abducted by men impersonating federal agents. This seems more than the act of a disturbed mind, Ms. Kitcheyan. We need your help to figure out what happened down there."

"I'm just a receiving clerk."

"And the only surviving member of your department and, apparently, still in danger, judging from the fact that the two men who abducted you yesterday are still at large. And that happened right here in the safety of your reservation. You need protection, Amber."

She set her jaw and tipped her chin down and looked away. Forrest sighed. Then he continued.

"What if one of these men is killed trying to protect you?"

That hit home. She couldn't bear that.

"And if you refuse to cooperate, we will take you into custody."

Carter stepped in. "You can't remove her from our tribal land."

"I can because she is no longer a member of the Turquoise Canyon Tribe. Her membership was rescinded years ago."

Carter's shoulders sank, and Amber braced. It hadn't taken them long to discover her weakness.

"You can't take my brother," said Jack Bear Den.

"True. But we are requesting he accompany us."

"I don't give a flying fart what you are requesting," said Jack.

Carter pressed a hand to his Jack's beefy forearm, and the two brothers shared a long look.

"Carter, no," said Jack.

Carter drew a long breath and let it go. "I'm not leaving her."

Jack stared up at the ceiling and then back at his brother. "She had no trouble leaving you."

Amber felt small and hollow. Brittle as burned paper in the wind. She *had* left him. Saving him from trying to protect her yet again. Perhaps she could do the same today. She believed Carter still had feelings for her and was still trying to solve all her problems. Did he see her as another friend thrown from safety into danger? She prayed she wasn't his chance for redemption. His charity would be worse than his contempt.

It had been so hard to walk away last time. But no worse than marrying a man who did not listen to or trust her. She still didn't know if she had been right to go. It seemed the only way. Maybe she should have tried harder.

She turned to face Carter.

"I don't want you to come," said Amber, her voice soft and low but somehow resonating like a gunshot in the quiet room.

"Well, too damn bad. This time *I* get to choose, and I'm not letting you go alone."

"I need time to think," she said, stalling.

Forrest's expression was sympathetic. "I've read your initial statements, but I have some questions to ask in the examination room with Chief Tinnin before we go. And you are going, Ms. Kitcheyan," said Agent Forrest. "We'll be ready in just a minute."

The men moved to the far side of the squad room. Carter hesitated, lingering a few steps from her, looking back, and then joined the others.

A minute. She pressed both hands to her ears as the screaming voice of her own protests seemed to shriek inside her head like the rushing winds of a winter storm. She was going into protective custody with Carter Bear Den. For how long?

Then she thought of the shooting at her office. Her friends and colleagues. Didn't she have an obligation to help catch this man and then help convict him so he could never do such a thing again?

Forrest said he thought this shooting was more than the act of a disturbed mind. What did that mean? The man must be crazy.

But if he were crazy, then why was he so hard to find? Crazy people were not careful or organized. They were sloppy, impulsive. She certainly knew that. Crazy people were erratic. They might throw a television from its stand for no reason and then walk over broken shards with bare feet. Might fall asleep while driving or forget to pick you up at school. They might throw things at you when angry. Amber lifted a hand to her lip and then forced it down with the memories. The pulsing in her heart ached all the way up to her throat.

Why couldn't they catch the shooter?

Because Agent Forrest was correct. This man wasn't crazy. He was sane, and he was after her. The realization made her sway. Carter left the three men in their discussion and hurried to her.

"Amber, I've got you."

"Don't do this. Let me go."

"You are not getting away from me this time. We have business to settle, and if we have to be locked in protective custody to settle it, that's what we'll do."

Chapter Twelve

A few minutes later, Amber sat facing the closed door in the windowless interrogation room. Chief Tinnin and Forrest sat across from her and had brought her a glass of water. It was the only thing on the surface except for the FBI agent's laptop and a digital tape recorder with a glowing red eye. Recording.

Amber had fought back against the fear, pushing it down deep again. After this interview, they were taking her into custody. She looked at the two armed men and recognized she was already in custody.

Should she call her mother? Her father? She winced at that thought. Her father's words came back like a promise.

Listen, you, I run this family. You do what you're told or else.

Once he had disowned her, leaving had been her only choice. She had not thought he could do anything more to her once she was gone. How wrong she had been. He had still taken one thing more. And now here she sat. Powerless because of that theft.

Forrest looked up from his laptop, fingers poised. "Ready?"

She began where he asked her, before coming to

work, and ran through the entire day. Forrest did not interrupt or ask questions as the other two agents yesterday had done. He just listened until she fell silent.

"Could you give me the full names of the men who held you overnight?"

"They didn't hold me."

"Their names?"

Amber closed her mouth and looked away. She was not getting Ray or Dylan in trouble if she could help it.

"Ray Strong. Dylan Tehauno and the Bear Den twins," said Tinnin.

Amber's exhale was audible. Forrest's fingers tapped away on his laptop. Then he fixed those light brown eyes on her.

"Is there any reason that you can think of that your department might be targeted?"

That was the question Carter had asked her.

"Do crazy people need to have a reason?"

"Always."

"Maybe it was just random." Her churning stomach said otherwise.

"Doesn't appear random. Targeted and very specific."

"Targeted," said Amber. "Because he killed everyone at my office and then went after my supervisor."

"And then tried to kill you. Two attempts," said Forrest.

That assertion made her flesh crawl, and she rubbed her hands up and down her arms.

"Those guys yesterday were different men. I would have recognized the man who came after me in Lilac."

"Yes." He flipped through his notes. "But what

about the driver at Lilac. The guy with the blond hair and ball cap. Could that have been a wig?"

She thought back at the straw-like hair poking out from the cap.

"I only saw him for a second."

"And the driver in the glasses. You said he looked familiar. Same guy?"

She tried to think. "I'm not sure."

"But you saw him before?"

"Somewhere. Yes, I think so."

Forrest pushed aside his laptop and leaned toward her. "Amber, what has been going on in your office? Has there been anything unusual?"

She shook her head, not wanting to take this road with him. It was too terrible.

"I don't know."

"You were there when they shot Ibsen. What did you see?"

"I didn't see anything. I was outside his house."

"Did you hear anything?"

"Shots."

"Anything else?"

The question jarred her back. She had been standing before his home, her keys in her hand. She'd heard Ibsen.

I told you everything. I reported it, for God's sake. I told you we had a problem.

"Yes," she whispered. "My boss. He was shouting. He said he reported the problem."

"What did he say exactly?" asked Forrest.

"'I reported it. Told you there was a problem,'" she said, her eyes fixed on the field agent as the room seemed to spin.

"What problem, Amber?"

"I don't know."

"Think. Some detail that might be dangerous to someone."

"Yes, I…" She needed to remember. "I found something. An error on a delivery."

Forrest's eyes glittered like a hawk sighting prey. "When?"

"Monday's delivery. I brought the packing slip to…" She pressed her hand to her mouth as she seemed to hear her boss's voice begging for his life. The problem. Was it her? She squeezed her eyes shut and then forced her hand away from her mouth and continued. "I brought it to Harvey Ibsen's attention Monday afternoon. I thought he'd want to check the shipment Tuesday, but…" She shook her head. "But he… But…" Her gaze shifted as she stretched back to Monday. He'd hurried her out of his office before she even had time to point out the error. She had considered going back in his office, but he'd been on the phone. Then Tuesday morning he'd been ill. Or said he was ill.

"But what, Amber?"

"But he was sick. Right after I told him that I noticed that the slip and the shipments didn't match. I brought it to him, and he said he'd handle it."

"When?"

"Monday." She pressed both hands to her cheeks.

"The day before the shooting," Forrest clarified. "That Monday?"

She looked at him with widening eyes. "Was it me? Did I cause this?"

Forrest's alert stare gave her no comfort.

"What happened Monday?" he asked.

"I give the packing slip to Nancy once I've checked it. But usually that's after it's already unloaded by our guys. They put the boxes away, and I count the contents. You know. That's what I do."

"How was this different?"

"I met the truck because Mr. Ibsen was unavailable."

"What was the error you spotted?"

"I just check in the shipments. That's it. Ten boxes of this. Four cartons of that. But Ibsen wasn't there to talk to the driver this time. He gave me the PO to sign. I'm not allowed to do that. So I made the driver wait and took it to Mr. Ibsen. On the way I saw that the two didn't match."

"The purchase order and the packing slip?" asked Forrest.

"That's right. I told Mr. Ibsen, and he…seemed anxious, took both the PO and packing slip before I could even explain what the problem was and told me to get back to work. So I did."

Ibsen had escorted her from his office, and she had gone. But she'd stopped before his open door, thinking she had not shown him the actual overage. She'd lingered there, trying to decide if she should go back in there, so she had heard him place a call and ask for a Mr. Theron Wrangler. He'd paused and then told someone it was urgent and to have Wrangler call him ASAP. An instant later, Ibsen had appeared at his office door, spotted her loitering and turned purple, shouting at her to get back to work.

"What was the problem?" asked Forrest. "They didn't match? Were things missing?"

"No, a surplus. More in the delivery than in the purchase order."

"What was in the order?" asked Forrest.

"Blasting material mostly. Chemicals, and I don't know exactly." Amber's throat went dry as implications she had not considered came to her like a blast in the copper mine. *Explosives.* More delivered than checked in. What was happening to the extra? She wasn't in charge of inventory. That was Ibsen's job.

Amber sat back in her chair, staring out with sightless eyes as she remembered the exchange and how Harvey had kept wiping his mouth with the palm of his hand.

"But you saw the discrepancy. How much and of what, exactly?"

She told him the chemicals and supplies that she recalled and the quantities on both slips. Agent Forrest sat back in his chair.

"Are you familiar with an organization called BEAR?"

Tinnin's glance shot from Forrest to her, and she thought that the chief had heard of BEAR. The chief shifted, and a finger went under the collar of his shirt.

"Or one named WOLF?" asked Forrest.

"The agents who questioned me yesterday mentioned them. I didn't know them. I've asked about them since."

She frowned, trying to understand what this had to do with the shooting.

"Amber, your father is a member of PAN. So is your uncle Kenshaw Little Falcon."

"Lots of people are. PAN—Protecting All Nature. They're pacifists. I even joined the rally to save Mesa Summit when I was a freshmen at Turquoise Canyon High."

"Yes, I know."

She frowned. "It's an environmental organization. Preserving wild places and protecting habitats."

Forrest looked skeptical. She was at a loss as to what he wanted from her.

"PAN has ties to both WOLF and BEAR. Those are ecoterrorist groups. Radical branches of PAN."

She met his hawkish eyes. "I don't understand. Were they protesting the mine?" It wouldn't be the first time. Her mother had told her how upset her father had been at learning the name of her latest employer.

Her skin tingled, and her ears buzzed. This didn't seem real. She shook her head in denial.

It wasn't a mistake—none of it.

The explosives, she thought. Where were they? Who had them?

Forrest's phone buzzed. He retrieved the mobile and glanced at the screen. Then he closed his laptop.

"Transport is ready," he said.

Chapter Thirteen

Amber did not get a chance to speak to Carter when she left the interrogation room. They ate lunch separately, as he was in the midst of being questioned.

Finally, as the afternoon gave way to evening and the sun cast the mountains in hard angles of blue and pink, they were transported in a van, with tribal and federal escort vehicles, off the reservation to a hotel suite where they would stay until the following morning when they would be transferred to the custody of US Marshals.

Agent Forrest introduced the FBI agents, Rose and Decker, who would be protecting them, and then left to continue the search for the shooter and accomplices. Amber shook hands with their babysitters. Both had similar suits, sidearms, precision haircuts, hawkish eyes and clean-shaven jaws. But there were differences. Rose's hair was two shades lighter brown than Decker's and, while Decker had the lean body of a runner, Rose was shorter and broader across the chest.

They were marched to the elevator and rode to the top floor, six, and then marched down a garish carpet to their suite. There was an outer door. Beyond lay an alcove and two more doors. They were admitted to the first by key card. Amber found a small kitchenette with tile floor and a table with two chairs.

The FBI agents followed, and the room became small with five of them crowded in an awkward circle.

Forrest gave final instructions and said his farewells. The door clicked shut behind them, and Amber's skin began to itch. It was as if the walls were closing in around her.

Decker took a seat on the couch and opened his laptop. Rose stepped out after Forrest, presumably to take a position in the hall.

She blinked at Carter. "Want to pick a bedroom?"

The thought of Carter and bedrooms made her insides turn to goo. Her energy, which had dwindled, made a rapid return, causing her to tingle in all the wrong places.

She swallowed in disgust and gave herself a silent talking-to. This man had come to protect her. She appreciated it but agreed with his twin. Carter should have stayed on the reservation. And nothing had changed between them. She passed him and his outstretched arm and headed out of the kitchenette and she discovered another sitting room with long red couch and recliner facing a large flat-screen television.

Carter paused behind her. "All the movies we can watch."

Sitting beside Carter on that wide couch watching movies did not sound like a very good idea. Just being alone with him made her entire body twitch. The last time they'd been in a hotel together they had not been there to watch TV. She reined herself in.

They both explored the two bedrooms on opposite sides of the sitting room finding mirror images right down to the still-life prints of Acoma pottery on the wall. She dropped the small duffel Kay had packed on the king-size bed, claiming the second bedroom.

"I'm starving. You want anything?" he asked.

Amber shook her head. How could he think of food right now?

"You have to be hungry."

She was, and that annoyed her, as well.

"We can't leave," she reminded him, as if he had not been listening. Though, if she were inclined to run, now would be the time. She weighed her need for escape against her need to stay alive.

"I'll order something. One of Forrest's guys will pick it up."

"Fine."

Carter left for the kitchen, returning with a three-ring notebook holding an assortment of take-out menus to find Amber now in the living area. Carter flipped back and forth.

While he studied the menus, she studied him. His brother Jack had advised him against leaving the reservation, but he'd ignored him.

"Why didn't you listen to Jack?" she asked.

He lowered the binder and met her gaze.

"Because I want you safe."

"Why?"

He shrugged. "They say old feelings die hard."

She thought of his feelings for her. Not respect. Certainly not trust.

"What do you think love is, Carter?" she asked.

His brows came together, forming a hard line between them.

"Caring for someone else more than for yourself," he said. "Protecting them."

"I think it is about trust. Trusting another person with your vulnerabilities and your fears. Believing that person and believing *in* that person. Listening to them."

Now his brow wrinkled, and he cocked his head.

"I listen," he said.

"Do you?"

"Yes, and I forgive you for leaving the tribe, Amber."

She stood and stepped past him. She had cleared her bedroom door and had a hand on the knob when he called to her.

"Amber, please. Come back."

Instead she closed the door between them.

Amber lay on the pristine coverlet and tried to rest, but she was so angry at Carter.

He forgave her.

She could walk right back in there and explain everything to him. But she wouldn't. She was doubly infuriated that he would forgive her for something she would never do and that he could ever believe she would give up her membership in her tribe in the first place. Did he know her so little that he would believe she would voluntarily relinquish who she was? Clearly, he did because he had accepted her father's word and believed him without even speaking about it with the woman he claimed to love. This entire thing only made it more apparent why she couldn't be with him. He didn't know her or trust her.

So why did she want him still?

There was a gentle knock on her door. She squeezed her eyes shut, then cleared her throat, but the lump remained firmly lodged in place.

"Come in."

The door eased open, and Carter peeked inside. The sky had gone dark, and she must have seemed just an outline on the wide white bedspread.

"I ordered something."

"Thank you."

"Can I come in?"

It was a bad idea. She rolled to her side and pushed the button that illuminated the bedside lamp. Then she motioned him in. He sat beside her on the bed, sagging as if exhausted.

She felt pity then. He'd left their people to help her, and she had sniped at him.

"I'm sorry, Amber. I just don't understand what I did."

And to explain it was to have to ask for what should be hers by right. If he loved her, the respect and trust were just branches of the same tree.

"I know."

"Can we talk while we're waiting for dinner?" he asked.

"Sure."

She pushed up to an elbow and rested a hand on his shoulder. Amber had meant the touch to be comforting, but even through the fabric of his soft cotton shirt the heat scorched her, and the tingling tension jolted up her nerves like a pulse of electricity. She glanced up to see Carter's complete stillness. The muscles beneath her hand bunched as he turned to look down at her. His Adam's apple bobbed, and his tongue dipped to drag back and forth along his lower lip.

The action sent a quick-fire explosion through her body. Her skin tingled, and her heart thudded. This, at least, had never changed between them. She still wanted him, and the need was growing unbearable.

He assessed her, his eyes dipping to take a leisurely perusal of her body. She felt his glance as a physical thing. Her stomach muscles tightened, and she lifted to an extended arm, drawn closer by her need and this desire.

This was bad.

Carter brushed the loose wisps of hair from her face. Then lifted her chin between his thumb and curved index finger. His hand was warm and his grip steady.

He dipped, angling his head for a kiss, and she lifted her chin to meet him. Their mouths pressed together. This was no gentle coaxing seduction. This kiss felt different in every way. It was powerful and possessive. Her mind went cloudy as her resistance dissolved like honey in hot water.

She pressed forward, falling against him, her breasts tingling with the contact of the hard muscle of his chest as strong arms enfolded her.

He broke the kiss and held her. She lifted her arms to hold him, too.

They had been through so much together in the past and in the last three days.

"You still taste like mint," he whispered and nipped her ear.

She shivered with pleasure and raked her fingers over his back. From the hall, she heard a beep, and Carter set her aside. The outer door clicked, and the two agents spoke. The Anglo agent was back.

A moment later Rose stood in her open door, holding a large paper bag as he peered into the dark room "Dinner is here. You two want to eat out here or in the kitchen?" asked Rose.

"Living room," she replied.

Amber wondered if her mouth looked as puffy as it felt. It had been a while since anyone had kissed her like that.

"You two all right?" asked Rose.

"Yeah. Coming." Carter stood and offered a hand. Amber flushed and accepted it, allowing him to guide her from the bed, but she glanced back and wondered. The object of her hunger had changed from food to the man guiding her along.

Rose left them with the two bags that contained dinner, which Carter unpacked. Amber settled in the chair, and Carter took the couch. Carter offered a prayer of thanks before they ate, and she added her own. The food was Thai and better than she expected.

"What will happen now?" she asked.

"You mean after dinner?"

She tried for a smile, but the worry ate her up. Carter gave her his best guess on what the police and FBI were doing. He could not tell her how long they would be caged up.

"Will I have to go back to Lilac?" she asked.

He pressed his enticing mouth together and shook his head.

"I doubt it."

"I'm a suspect, right?"

"Did you do anything wrong?" he asked.

"I did not. But they asked me about organizations called BEAR and WOLF."

Carter set aside his noodle dish.

"Do you know them?" she asked.

"One of them." He looked worried. "WOLF stands for the *Warriors Of Land Forever*. They'd be interested in a pit mine. That group damages property, spiking trees marked for logging. That kind of thing. Might attack anything that invades wild places."

That didn't sound good.

"What about BEAR?"

"Never heard of them." He returned his attention to his plate, but he seemed distracted now.

"They knew I'd been at a PAN protest." She ate more of the jasmine rice and mixed veggies, having already devoured all the chicken. "Should I be worried?"

He didn't say no. She set aside her plate, her appetite spoiled. He offered her some of his, and she declined.

"Should I ask for a lawyer?" she asked, already wondering where and how to locate someone.

"You haven't been arrested or charged. You're in custody as a witness. Right now you just need to rest and eat." He motioned to her half-eaten supper.

She nodded her acceptance.

Rose stepped into the doorway. "Everything come out all right?"

"Like having a butler," she murmured in Apache.

"Until you try to leave," said Carter.

"You two need anything else?" asked the agent.

"Books," said Amber.

"Music," said Carter.

Rose nodded, reversed course and disappeared through the doorway.

"Would they tell us if they caught them?" she asked.

Carter finished his meal and sat back. "Yes. I think they would."

"So they haven't even caught the shooter. It's been days."

"They will. FBI. State police, sheriffs and local police are all on it."

"What if they don't?"

He gave her a long look, and she wondered if he understood. She was the target. What if they couldn't find the men trying to kill her?

"I can't stay here forever."

"Be patient. We both need some rest. Tomorrow things will be better."

CARTER WISHED AMBER would eat a little more. He also wished there was more he could do to assure her, but honestly he could not fathom how the gunman had evaded the police this long.

He found himself staring at her mouth, recalling their kiss, and had to shake himself back to attention.

He ignored the thrumming need that she stirred inside him as he collected the leftovers. They both carried the packaging out to the kitchen and returned to the living area couch.

Sated by food, a more insistent hunger continued to gnaw at him.

"Want to watch TV?" he asked.

She shook her head. "I'm afraid of the scroll bar. I don't want to see the body count or, worse, video footage of the Lilac Mine."

Their gazes met, and the pulsing ache that had been in his chest moved south.

"You're staring at me." She used one finger to trace the outline of the scar on her lip. "It's this, isn't it?"

"I'll admit being attracted to your mouth forever, but I was wondering about that scar. You had it when you visited me when I was recuperating. But not before that. What happened?"

She flushed, her gaze dropped to her lap, and she closed her eyes. "Finally the right question," she whispered.

"What?"

"You didn't ask me how I cut it or what I did. You asked me what happened."

"Yes."

Amber pressed her lips together, making the scar turn from pink to white.

"My dad did this the day he disowned me."

Fury surged. Her father did that? He shook his head, wanting to deny it, knowing he couldn't. It took a moment to find his voice; he was so stunned at her revelation.

"He told me you left."

"I know. What I never understood was why you believed him."

He tried to catch up.

"Why didn't you tell me?"

"I did. I went to you the minute I found out about the credit fraud, and you told me that everything I owned was his."

He had said that, hadn't he?

"Then you told me to go home and that you'd take care of everything."

"I would have," he said.

"No. Some things you can't fix. Sometimes you just

have to listen and believe that the one you love knows what she is talking about."

"But you…" He checked himself at the narrowing of her eyes. He had been about to say that she had broken the engagement and follow that by reminding her that she had left them all. But he saw something in that cold, impassive stare, some warning that he was about to make another mistake. He couldn't afford to lose her again.

"Nine years. You've been gone nine years."

"Yes."

"And I never understood why."

"So ask me."

Now his eyes narrowed. "I did ask you."

"No, you asked me why I rescinded my membership in the tribe. Why I broke our engagement and why I left you." She fingered the scar. "You asked me *why* I did things. You never asked me what happened. Not once."

"I know what happened."

"Do you? Or do you only know one side of a story?"

Her father's side. Now he understood what she meant. Her father had come to him first. Explained things, and he had accepted Manny Kitcheyan's word out of respect. Had that tainted his objectivity? For a minute it felt like his first jump from an airplane, as the world rushed closer and his stomach pressed up where his lungs should be. Had he done that to her?

He sat back on the couch, his hand pressed over his mouth as he stared. Finally he dragged his hand away and squeeze it into a fist.

"Amber, are you telling me you left because I asked the wrong question?"

"Yes."

He shifted to face her and hesitated. "What happened, Amber?"

Amber moved to sit beside Carter on the couch. He knew that what she was about to say was important and so he struggled to listen. But inside his head a voice was screaming, *the wrong question. All this time and she left because I asked the wrong question.*

He kept his face impassive, but inside a tempest swirled. He feared the power of the storm. She folded an ankle under her thigh and turned so that she sat sideways to face him.

"My father was there before me. Wasn't he?"

Carter nodded, not trusting his voice.

"I'm sure he told you I was making a big thing out of nothing."

"It was just a truck, Amber."

"No. Not just."

His impulse was to remind her that he had offered to pay for the damned thing, but instead, he kept his mouth shut. Her father's new red truck. The one that overextended the family budget and triggered the fight between him and Amber. He recalled the day she'd come to him and said she wanted to get married right that very minute. He had laughed, not realizing how serious she had been. He'd tried to send her home to apologize, to finish high school and start community college. When he told her he'd already given her father the signing bonus she went crazy and said she was going to the police.

He recalled exactly what he had said then. *As long as we're engaged, I am a part of this family.*

She had removed his ring, held it out to him. "I won't marry you."

"Don't be silly. You're not serious."

"Will you change your mind about the signing bonus?" she asked.

He narrowed his eyes. *"No."*

She offered his ring.

"This is childish, Amber."

"Childish?" She offered the ring. *"Take it."*

"No."

Carter swallowed, met her steady gaze. "Was it because I called you childish?"

"Partly. You wouldn't listen. Had already made up your mind what to do without consulting me. I could see it then. Going from my father's control to yours. You even said to me that I would be theirs until we married, and then I'd be yours."

He blinked at her. "So what did your father do that was so terrible?"

She pressed her lips together, making the scar turn from pink to white.

"My dad did this the day I left. Threw a beer bottle at me."

A cold knife blade of dread pierced his heart. He gently held her chin, turning her head from side to side as he looked at the tiny white crescent. Now he recognized the pressure cut of her tooth where it had sliced through the soft tissue of her upper lip.

"I didn't know he hit you," said Carter.

"He never did. And this was the only time he did something like this. But what else he did was worse."

Carter released her jaw and braced for the truth that he would not even consider when he was a young man.

"Tell me," he said.

And she did. She told him about the debt her father accumulated by gambling and buying things they did not need. About how, with her parents' credit in shambles, he had turned to his daughters' and stolen their identity.

"It was nearly seventy thousand dollars when I found out."

When she had gone to him about the money for the truck, she should have made him understand. Or was it that he should have listened instead of dismissing her concerns?

"He stole from me and Kay and Ellie. Ellie was eleven years old, and he charged thirteen thousand dollars in her name."

"You should have told me."

"I told you. I said he stole from us. That he had credit cards in our names. You told me to go back home and smooth things over, apologize and let you handle it. You patted me on the head. I had to go to the tribal police. Do you know what they said?"

He shook his head.

"Two choices. Either I accepted the debt as my own, or I filed charges against my father for identity theft. Then they would press charges, and he would be arrested and serve jail time."

"Or declare bankruptcy?"

"Seventeen-year-olds can't do that. I am still angry at my father, but he is my father. I could not have him arrested, embarrassed before everyone he knows. So I shut down all lines of credit. A man in Darabee with credit counseling helped me. But I couldn't restructure the debt until I was eighteen, and no one would give me a loan."

"You took this all on yourself?" Carter's stomach ached from the thought of her carrying this burden. Her eyes showed the betrayal she felt from her father, from him.

"Yes. Eventually it went to debt collectors. That's why I don't carry a mobile phone. They call all the time, and they are so terrible. I've been settling the balances bit by bit. But when my dad learned what I did—" she tapped her upper lip "—he gave me this and threw me out."

"You should have…" He stopped. She had come to him, twice. He'd sent her back home.

"I wish you had told me what he did."

"I didn't know how bad it was yet. Then you went to basic, and I got a bill from a credit card company. This had been going on for years."

"I didn't understand."

"I don't know if this makes any sense, but I wanted to protect my father, and I wanted to protect you."

"I loved you then, Amber. I would have done anything for you."

"Except what I needed most. I wasn't a child, then, and I wasn't willing to be a wife of a man who treated me like one."

"I tried to solve it."

"I never asked you to. But I did ask you to listen. To trust me. Believe that if I said it was important, then it was important."

He met her gaze, seeing the glimmer of eyes filling with tears. They fell from her lower lids, dropping all the way to her lap.

He took her hand and squeezed. "Amber, please... I'm so sorry."

She smiled as the tears continued to fall. "I'm so glad."

He had another apology to make. Amber had come back to see him once, when he'd been home recovering from his injuries. She'd met him on his parents' porch on a sunny August day when his arm was still bandaged.

"Amber, about that day in August when you came to see me."

She drew her hand away and used it to wiped at her eyes, which filled up almost instantly.

"Yeager had been captured. They took him in May. We got notification of a proof of life video that December. It was terrible. We all felt so guilty for leaving him."

"You couldn't get to him," she said.

He made a face. "Anyway, Jack was a tribal police patrolman then. He told me you relinquished your membership, and it made me so mad. But now..." Now he wasn't certain. He no longer trusted what he had heard.

He stared at her, so familiar and yet now a stranger. She was so beautiful, even in grief. Had he misjudged her twice? "Amber, what happened?"

"My dad again. I didn't even know until you told me. I thought it was a mistake. But when I went home, my mother admitted what he had done, withdrawn his oldest child from our tribe. He did that on the day he disowned me."

"You didn't leave?"

She shook her head. "They're my people."

Her father had stolen her identity in more ways than one.

"We have to fix this," he said.

"Why? I'm going to be in protective custody."

"That's temporary," he said.

She drew a long breath. "Maybe."

Carter stood. "I have to call Jack."

Chapter Fourteen

Carter had to speak to the FBI before using his mobile, but they allowed him to call his brother. It was a sharp reminder of what he'd be facing when he went with Amber tomorrow. He'd be cut off from his family and his tribe. But Amber's safety now seemed more important than all that.

He asked his brother to look into the tribe's policy for reestablishing membership because he thought he'd seen something on their website about minor children. His brother promised to check.

Jack relayed some news about the case. The shooter and driver were still at large, but they now knew how the inside man had gained access to the Lilac administration building.

"I want to see you tomorrow morning," said Jack.

Carter knew it might be his last contact with anyone in his family until after the killers were apprehended. He thought about his mom and dad and brothers all at that dinner the night the tribe had kept them safe. His throat constricted.

"Yeah. I'd like that."

"I'll bring you some of your stuff. See you tomorrow, brother."

Carter gave the phone to Agent Rose and returned to Amber, finding her staring blankly at the television which was still off. He had the job of telling Amber that the inside man had used a stolen security key card from one of the Lilac Mine employees to gain access to her building. She stared at him wide-eyed as he told her of the development in the case.

"But how did he get Ann-Marie's card?" Her hands went to her mouth, and she spoke from behind them. "She's not involved in this. Is she?"

"She didn't do anything wrong," he said.

Amber blew out a breath, and he hated that he had to tell her the rest.

"But whoever stole her card also killed her."

Her eyes filled with tears as she shook her head in denial. "Killed her? But…but he didn't need to kill her. He could have just tied her up or…" The sobs stopped the rest.

Carter pulled her close.

Amber met his gaze as she struggled to speak past the flood of tears. "She saw his face. Just like us."

Now her hands covered her eyes as she rocked back and forth against him.

Carter drew her into his lap, and her tears soaked the collar of his shirt.

"I'll keep you safe, Amber. I swear I will."

She clung, and he stroked her head and rubbed her back. At last, her tears stopped, and her breathing changed. He rocked her like a child as she fell asleep and then gently carried her to bed. She woke as he tucked her legs beneath the coverlet.

"What time is it?" she asked.

"After midnight."

"Tomorrow already," she muttered.

"Yes."

"Taking us tomorrow." Her words were slurred as she fought the sleep that held her.

He stood over her for a moment, wishing he could stay with her.

"Carter?"

"Yes?"

She pushed over on the mattress and lay an open hand beside her. Amber's eyes remained half closed as she cast him a sultry look. But it was exhaustion, he knew. Not flirtation, so he reined in his roaring need.

"Could you hold me for a while?"

Carter hesitated at her request. "I don't think that's such a great idea."

"Just a few minutes. Please?"

She didn't want him in the way he wanted her. But perhaps she forgave him for not understanding how to correctly honor a wife. He sat on the edge of her bed.

"I'm here," he said.

He glanced at the open door and the light spilling across the industrial carpet. Then he thought of the agents in the other room.

She slid under the covers and across to the middle of the gigantic bed. Carter eased down beside her, already regretting his decision.

Amber rolled to her side and snuggled up against him, cuddling his biceps so that his muscle rested against the soft pillow of her breasts. He exhaled through his teeth and squeezed his eyes shut, thankful for the relentless air-conditioning that cooled his fevered skin. But not the longing. That burned too hot. She was different than all women since—and not just because she was his first. She was also his only, at least in his heart. There had been others since she'd left him. He'd tried and failed to move on. But he never could. Now he understood why. None of them were Amber.

"Thank you," she whispered.

"Just until you fall asleep. Okay?" After that he would need some alone time and a shower.

"'Kay," she breathed on a sigh.

Her grip eased and her mouth parted.

Carter laced his fingers together across his stomach and concentrated on his breathing. Amber rolled to her back. He saw his chance and took it, easing off the mattress.

He stood at her bedside, thinking of all the days and nights they had missed and wanting a second chance. They were different people now. His feelings for her were strong but tangled like fishing line on a low branch. He didn't know how to untie the knots. She had wanted him to have faith in her. Instead he had diminished all her concerns. He hadn't taken them, or her, seriously. What an ass he had been. But was he willing to open himself up to that kind of hurt again?

She'd left him once. She could do it again, and just like last time he wouldn't understand, couldn't understand. If she loved him, she would have stayed.

He returned to his room. He would protect her. But he wasn't going to give her his heart—not again.

CARTER DID NOT sleep well and was on his second cup of coffee when Detective Jack Bear Den was admitted to their suite the following morning.

Jack wore his usual work attire: boots, jeans, shirt and a blazer. He removed his white cowboy hat, and the brothers exchanged a hug. When they parted, Jack handed over the document Carter had requested.

"Signed by her parents. Just as you suspected."

Carter glanced over the copy of the notarized document that Amber had not signed. Joy mingled with dismay to find exactly what Amber had told him. He should have known this without the proof. Should have believed in her.

"What a jerk," he muttered.

"Yeah, he is," agreed Jack, clearly thinking of Amber's father, Manny. Somehow what Carter had done felt worse.

Amber would no more give up her heritage than he would. Carter's head hung in shame. She'd been protecting her parents at her expense.

Carter looked at her father's signature and knew that Manny Kitcheyan had done this out of malice. To punish his daughter for thwarting him.

Jack pointed to the paper. "She was supposed to sign it because she was over fifteen. Don't know how that slipped by because her birthday is right on the form."

Carter said a silent prayer. "Does that mean she can overturn it?"

"She can, and she doesn't need to mention what her father did, though why she wouldn't, I do not know."

"How?" asked Carter.

Jack reached in his breast pocket and retrieved a folded page. Then he read the pertinent section aloud.

"'Relinquishment of a Minor Child: In the case of a minor child under the age of eighteen years, the relinquishment statement must be signed by the guardian or both parents. If an enrolled member over eighteen years of age relinquishes membership...' Hold on, not that part." Jack scanned. "Here. 'However, if the enrolled member was under eighteen years of age at the time of relinquishment, said person may reapply for enrollment upon reaching the age of eighteen.'" Jack lifted his gaze in triumph. "She's in if she wants in."

Carter hugged him. Jack thumped his back and then drew away to hand over the two pages.

Jack's smile wavered, and his jaw ticking revealed that he had something more.

He turned to Carter and motioned with his head for him to follow. Carter excused them and trailed Jack to the living area.

Jack paused just inside the doorway and faced Carter. He toyed with the turquoise ring on his middle finger, twisting it from side to side. "First, Dylan and Ray checked in. They saw our shaman. He says he sent you because he wanted you and Amber to have a chance to reconcile. Said it was your destinies."

Carter's brow furrowed. "What about the timing?"

Jack shrugged. "He's saying coincidence."

Carter made a face. "You buy that?"

Jack shook his head. "Million to one. Listen, Tinnin told me to tell you that the US Marshals are taking custody of you and Amber around nine."

Carter glanced at the clock on the DVD player. It was just past seven in the morning.

The brothers exchanged a long, silent look. Carter's breathing picked up with his heart rate. Jack's face was paler than he'd ever seen it.

"Best guess?" asked Carter.

Jack shook his head and swallowed. "When they catch him and they will, we will know better. If he's working alone, you'll be released."

"If he's not working alone?" Carter knew the drill, but still he wanted Jack to say it. To know in his heart that his world was really tipping.

"If those guys were sent here, as hit men on an assignment, it gets more complicated. They have to be sure that you are not at risk. If there is reason to think your lives are in danger, they'll offer you witness protection."

The words hit him like a blunt cleaver, making him wince. "I'd be gone for good."

Jack nodded. "If you take it. You can demand to be returned to the tribe, or I can take you out right now."

"What about Amber?"

"Once she's reinstated, she could do the same." Jack reached into his back pocket and handed over more documents. "Here's all she needs. A petition to reinstate."

"How long does this take?"

"Council meets every week." Jack twisted the ring all the way around his finger. "But you'll be in custody then. You still going with her?"

Carter said nothing, but Jack's expression told him that his brother knew his mind. His mournful look broke Carter's control. He rested a hand on Jack's shoulder. They no longer had the time he had expected. The years and years. With Amber's life in jeopardy and his, too, as her protector, Carter recognized that he might not always be here for Jack. He'd turned Jack down flat when he had first made his appeal. But what if Carter wasn't here to help him? Jack could go to Tommy or Kurt, he supposed, but it had been hard for Jack to ask him and they were twins. To ask his kid brothers would be even tougher. Carter felt in his heart that if he didn't do this, Jack would never get his answers. Never know the truth.

Carter switched to Apache. "You remember what you asked me? About the sibling test?"

A while back, Jack had wondered if Carter would be willing to take a DNA test that would show if they shared both parents. It was a way around asking Mom flat out if Jack had a different father.

"I remember."

"I'll take the test."

Jack nodded.

"Bring it soon."

Jack glanced back at the FBI agent who now stood in the doorway watching them, perhaps curious that they spoke in the language of their birth. Then he turned back to Carter.

"I did ask Mom about...you know."

Carter's eyes widened.

"What'd she say?"

"She said that she had never been with a man other than her husband."

Carter wanted to feel reassured, but Jack's gray eyes dared him to ignore what was staring him in the face. Jack's blood type, his skin tone, his wavy hair and the sheer size of him all told a different tale. In their youth, Carter had fought anyone who said Jack wasn't his brother. But in his heart the doubt grew.

"That means Mom is either a liar or I'm crazy," said Jack.

"Yeah. You believe her?" asked Carter.

"If I did, I wouldn't have asked you to take the sibling test."

Carter heard the shower turn on and glanced toward Amber's room. Had her sleep been as fitful as his?

He faced his brother and asked him if he'd ever heard of a group called BEAR. Jack had not but promised to check into it.

Jack tugged on his hat and then aimed a finger at the agent who was tall but not a male mountain like Jack. "You take care of my brother."

Chapter Fifteen

When Amber emerged from her bedroom in Kay's nightie and the hotel's plush terry-cloth robe, she found Carter at the door holding out a ceramic mug brimming with dark black coffee. She smiled in gratitude.

She tried to ignore the V of bronze male flesh revealed by his gaping cotton shirt when he extended his arm. Their fingers brushed in the exchange. Her reaction to his touch was harder to ignore. Her stomach twitched, and her eyes flashed to his. His brow quirked, and her face went hot. Carter cleared his throat.

"You slipped out last night," she said, cradling the cup.

"I said I would."

She smiled and inhaled the aroma of coffee.

"Jack stopped in. He said the marshals will be here soon."

She sipped the coffee. "Did he ask you to go with him?"

Carter rubbed his neck, and she had her answer.

"I'm not your responsibility anymore, you know?"

"I do know that." He didn't sound happy about it. "I need to see you through this, Amber."

"For old times' sake?"

He held her gaze as he gave his head a slow shake. "For now. Protecting you, I just have to. Not because you're a child or you aren't capable, but these are bad people, Amber. Really bad. Don't ask me to go."

She shook her head. "I won't. But I don't want you hurt because of me."

"I'm staying, Amber. Maybe we can figure this out together."

Did he mean what was happening or what was happening between them? Her heart accelerated as hope crept in. She took another sip of coffee. Carter twisted his fist into the palm of his opposite hand. It was a gesture she was becoming familiar with.

"I don't know how long they'll keep me. But I do know that, except for your time in the marines, you've lived in Turquoise Canyon your entire life. Your family is here. Your friends. Medicine society and your job. Everything you know. I don't want you to lose them because of me."

"I can understand that. But it won't be forever. Just until they catch these guys."

She wasn't sure. If these men who were after her were a part of a larger organization, WOLF or BEAR, then even if the FBI caught them, she might be in danger of retaliation. Certainly the authorities would keep her until the trial. That could be a long time.

She hung her head and let her hair fall over her face. What was she doing to him? She should tell him to go. But she couldn't.

Oh, no, she thought, not again. She was not going to fall in love with him again.

He brushed her hair back and lifted her chin with an index finger.

"You're lucky, Carter, to have people to come home to."

He cast her a sad smile that twisted her heart.

"I couldn't imagine a home where a parent would act like yours."

Her face and neck went hot. "It's shameful."

Carter locked his jaw, biting down until his jaw muscles pulsed. He was so angry at her father, her charming father who had glossed over all his failings and convinced Carter that Amber was just overreacting. She'd been more generous than he would have been, working nearly a decade to pay off her father's debts. She'd dropped out of school and even lost the chance to attend college.

"He should be in jail," said Carter.

She glanced at him. "Could you have sent your father to prison?"

He gave a tight shake of his head. They understood each other again. It felt strange. He tamped down the hope building inside him. She needed his protection. Had asked for nothing more. He'd made mistakes in the past, ones she found unforgivable and that he had not even known he had made. He didn't want to disappoint her again. But more than that, he didn't want her to leave him.

Agent Decker appeared in the doorway. "US Marshals are ten minutes out. Ms. Kitchcyan, get dressed, please."

Amber nodded.

Carter stroked her cheek. "We'll talk later."

She hoped so. Amber headed to her bathroom to

change. A few minutes later she emerged, wearing her sister's clothes. Kay had packed her skinny blue jeans and a gauzy white cotton blouse and a long gold-tone chain with clear crystals set every six inches or so. Kay's favorite, she knew. Her feet were clad in a stylish pair of walking shoes. She left off the denim jacket for now. Kay had remembered some bathroom items, but the only cosmetics were a pink lip gloss and citrus body spray. Amber used both. She tucked the lip gloss in a tight front pocket. Kay had included a dark blue wristlet with a gold clasp that Amber recognized had once belonged to Ellie. Amber fingered the pretty necklace and then touched the jeweled snap on the bag. Something from both of them. Amber smiled as her heart ached.

She told herself that she was not going to cry again. But when would she see her sisters again?

There was a knock at her door. She looped her hand through the wristlet, which was empty except for the body spray. Then she shouldered the small duffel.

"Coming."

She stepped from the room to find Carter waiting. He had braided his hair in one thick rope down his back. His shirt was a white oxford that was open at the collar to reveal a medicine bundle he had not been wearing earlier. Had Jack brought that in the bag he had given Carter yesterday?

His jeans included a brown leather belt with a turquoise buckle she knew Jack had been wearing yesterday. On his feet were hiking boots that looked well-worn. In his hand he held his overnight bag.

She pointed to the buckle. "Jack's?"

He nodded.

She lifted the necklace and then her wrist to show the bag. "Kay and Ellie."

"They're worried," he said.

With good reason, she thought.

He offered his arm, and she took it, glad for the warm reassurance of his body. He leaned down and sniffed.

"You smell good enough to eat."

"Uh-oh, and you're starving."

He chuckled. "Usually."

"You weren't wearing that medicine bundle before."

He glanced down at her. "You are very observant. My mother sent it. Thought I should wear it."

She knew that the contents of each man's medicine bundle was a private thing, and so she asked no more.

"I wish I had some sage and sweetgrass to burn. A prayer wouldn't hurt either."

Carter squeezed her hand, and they followed the agents out. They were escorted down in the service elevator and met the US marshals. There were two agents, one male and one female, Agent Pedro Mora Wells and his partner, Agent Eveline Landers. He was short, dark and already had a five-o'clock shadow. She was broad at the hips and shoulders and wore her hair in dangerous-looking, short bleached spikes. Her eyes were hidden behind oversize mirrored sunglasses.

The FBI walked them out through the laundry facility and into a white van that looked like the kind that hotels use as courtesy shuttles. Inside Amber found two rows of seats behind the front bucket seats. Carter helped her inside and then sat next to her in the center of the row. The marshals closed them in and then took their places in front, with Mora driving and Landers opposite. And they were off.

They drove through Darabee past the big box stores, fast-food chains, and occasional strip malls with restaurants and some shopping. Then they came to a familiar wooded stretch and passed the turnoff to their reservation. Carter's head swiveled as they passed an SUV she suspected Jack drove for work.

Amber sat back in the seat and gazed through windows catching glimpses of the azure waters of Antelope Lake, the last in the string of four bodies of water created by the damming of the Salt River. Two dams lay upstream from her reservation, including the largest, Alchesay, which held back Goodwin Lake and produced more electricity than the other three combined. Next came Skeleton Cliff Dam, Red Rock Dam and finally Mesa Salado which she could not see from the road. But she did see an Arizona State Police SUV sitting at the turnoff to Mesa Salado Dam.

They descended the mountain in a series of switchbacks for the next forty minutes. She watched the Douglas fir trees give way to pinyon pine. The appearance of agave signaled that they had returned to the lower elevations of arid rolling rock formations and the saguaro cacti. Here the road widened, becoming two lanes on each side.

The state police SUV pulled into the passing lane beside them, and Amber wondered briefly if it was the same one from up by Mesa Salado. An escort? She turned to look at them and noticed the passenger's window was open. Next she saw the passenger's face. *That face*—the face of the man leaving Harvey Ibsen's place.

She pointed as her words came out as a stammer. "The… That's him!"

"What?" said Carter, peering in the direction she pointed. The SUV now ran parallel to them, mimicking their speed. A rifle emerged from the passenger-side window.

"Gun!" shouted Carter.

Chapter Sixteen

Carter placed a broad hand on Amber's back and forced her forward as shots ripped through the vehicle's side panel. Marshal Mora slumped behind the wheel. Carter held Amber down with one hand and wrapped his other around his knees. The van veered, and the tires bogged as the front and back windshield shattered at once.

Landers screamed as they slid along the embankment. Carter straightened as the van left the road. Landers made a grab for the wheel as the van careened down an embankment and thundered on.

Mora flopped to the side, his body held erect by his shoulder restraint, his foot still evidently on the gas as they sped through the low scrub sending rocks knocking against the undercarriage.

Landers had one hand on her side and one on the wheel as she steered them perpendicular to the highway.

"Hold on!" she shouted.

Carter saw the scrub brush vanish, and the van tipped, sliding on the loose red sand, planting nose first into the ground. The rear tires remained at ground level and the front tires now rested on the floor of the arroyo, a dry river bed some three feet down.

"Out," said Landers.

Carter unfastened his belt, and Amber did the same. Carter reached forward, checking Mora's pulse at the neck and finding none.

Landers clutched her side, blood leaking between her fingers.

"I figure you have about a minute before they get here." The marshal spoke between clenched teeth. "Take his gun and phone."

Carter did as she suggested, finding his phone in his right pants pocket.

"Thirty seconds," she said, glancing back at him. "Run."

"What about you?" asked Amber.

"Lung shot. Can't run. Go."

Carter pulled open the van door and dragged Amber down beside him. He looked right and left down the wash. In either direction he could be out of sight in thirty seconds at a dead run.

He grabbed his duffel and pointed in the more difficult direction, the one with the denuded trees and rock.

"Run," he said.

Amber did run, and she was fast. Not as fast as he was but fast enough. In twenty seconds they were out of sight of the van. In a minute they were out of sight of the place where he had last seen the van.

They ran for another minute, and then he slowed them to a jog. They were both sweating and panting but not loud enough to miss the sound of the two gunshots.

Amber stilled, looking back. She didn't ask him, just stared in wide-eyed horror. He suspected that Agent Landers was dead.

"Who was it?" asked Carter.

"The man who killed Ibsen. The Lilac shooter." She glanced back at the way they had come. "He'll come after us. I know it."

"Maybe. Depends on how badly he wants to risk getting caught."

She stared at him, her breathing slowing rapidly back to normal. She was in good shape.

Amber glanced back over her shoulder in the way they had come.

"See anything?" she asked.

"No."

Amber grabbed the hem of her gauzy blouse and tugged the entire thing up over her head. Carter's attention snapped back to her.

"What are you doing?"

"It's white. Easy to see in this wash. We're rabbits. Brown is a much better color for hiding."

He was already unbuttoning his oxford as she stuffed her blouse in his duffel with her necklace.

He stowed his top in his green duffel, trying not to stare at her slim athletic figure and the lacy black bra that hugged her breasts.

"Come on," she said.

They ran again, a fast jog that took them over uneven ground and over rocks and tangled tree branches. He didn't stop, and she didn't ask him to. But over time her stride grew clumsy, and he slowed.

"They might follow or might go back to their vehicle to try to get ahead of us. This wash roughly parallels the road. I don't know when it might cross under the highway."

She had to pause as she spoke to catch her breath. "They might…go…the wrong way."

He nodded. Then he motioned to a section of the wash wall that had collapsed, offering some cover and also morning shade.

She followed as he tucked them in close to the earthen wall. He handed her back her blouse, and she shrugged into it. Next he offered water. She took very little.

Amber was a child of the arid Southwest who knew that water was precious. She returned the bottle, and he drank sparingly before returning it to his gear.

"What now?" she asked.

"We wait. If they show up first, we are in serious trouble. If it's the FBI or state police, we might be okay."

Amber looked up the narrow wash, topped with leafless brush, dry, yellowed grass and an occasional cactus.

"Too dangerous to continue."

"I think it will go under the road."

She peeked up over the earthen barrier at the way they had come.

"I hate to wait here like a sitting duck."

Carter lifted the marshal's gun. "Not defenseless."

Amber chose not to remind him that their attacker had used either an automatic or semiautomatic rifle.

"How did he find us again?" she asked.

"I don't know."

"He was waiting for us. I saw them parked in that state police vehicle way back in the turnoff for Mesa Salado Dam."

"Me, too."

"How did they know that we were in that van? The windows were tinted. They couldn't see us."

"Which is why they shot for the seats behind the driver," said Carter. His expression showed worry which made her more nervous.

"How did they get a state police vehicle?"

"I don't know. A copy, maybe."

"It fooled me." She glanced around at the thirsty trees that waited patiently for the July monsoons to fill the river.

"How long until the FBI find us?"

"Maybe an hour or two."

"You have cell phone service?" she asked.

He lifted out Mora's phone, an Android, and woke it up.

"Password protected," he said. He glanced at the emergency button but hesitated. Something felt wrong. "It's on. So the FBI can track us once they realize we're missing."

"Turn it off," she said.

He did.

"What are you thinking, Amber?" He trusted her, and her opinion mattered to him. She was smart, observant and completely aware of her surroundings. Any one of those attributes was rare enough.

She scrunched her forehead, making a single line form between her brows.

"If we were on the reservation, I'd say wait for help. But that was a state police vehicle."

"Or a copy."

"But it might be the real state police. So, what if we were picked up by FBI, and they weren't really FBI? Those guys at the tribal station told me they were Feds."

He settled back against the red earth wall behind them.

"I've been wondering about your question—how does that gunman get away?"

"And?"

"I think he has help."

That seemed obvious. But he felt she had more to say, so he didn't comment. They were both thinking it, but she was the one who finally came out and said it aloud.

"I hate to say it, but what kind of person can hide suspects, get inside information on the location of witnesses and then vanish again?"

He didn't like her train of thought but could not find a better explanation for what was happening to them.

She rested a hand on his knee. "Everything points to law enforcement personnel."

He set his jaw. If she was right, then waiting for help suddenly seemed a bad idea.

"Do you think they will let your brother know if you are missing?" she asked.

"I'm not sure. It is out of his jurisdiction."

"We should try to get to the reservation or to your brother."

She was right. Getting to Turquoise Canyon might be the only way to let their people know what had really happened. He knew for certain that tribal land was the one place on earth they might just be safe.

"You're right."

"But how? The reservation is at least seventy miles away and we don't have a vehicle or even a phone."

Chapter Seventeen

"They might be back there, waiting for us," he said.

"Risky to hang around, especially in a state police car. Assuming they are not state police, another trooper will definitely stop if he sees that SUV."

"Could be a while."

"You think they are still there?" she asked.

"Not sure. But there might be something useful in the van. They had a radio."

"No radios," said Amber. "We can call your brother if we get to a landline."

They made their way back to the van over the next hour, stopping to listen and scout. Once at the van they found both agents dead.

Carter looked at the bullet holes that told him that if Amber had not spotted the gunman the instant she had, they would both be dead, as well.

"You saved our lives," he said.

"No. I just pointed. You are the one who pushed us down below the path of the bullets."

Carter took a slow walk around the van, looking at the ground. Many of the Apache people were excellent trackers, and she knew Carter had this skill.

He confirmed her suspicion a moment later.

"Two men. Both in boots. One is about one-eighty and the other slighter, maybe one-fifty. They jogged down to the van and stopped there." He pointed to the place beside Mora.

Was that where they took the shot that killed Landers? she wondered.

"The smaller one circled the van around the back. He went slow, and he stopped at the door. They followed us to the river channel but went no farther. Then they both walked back up the bank."

She held her arms folded over her body as the cold reality of this situation chilled her heart.

"Did you see if they wore police uniforms?" he asked.

"I didn't notice."

"I'm going to take her gun. Look around and see if there is anything else worth carrying."

Amber searched the van and found a half consumed bottle of green tea and took that. Carter returned Mora's phone to his pocket and took Landers's service weapon.

"I have to go back to the road," he said.

"Why?"

"I need to leave a marker for my brothers."

She didn't know if he meant his actual brothers or members of his tribe. But it didn't matter.

"It's dangerous. You will be seen by passing cars."

"I'll be careful."

She nodded, and he gave her a swift kiss before jogging away. Amber pressed her fingers to her lips. His kiss was quick and possessive. She watched him go and then saw him drop to the ground, waiting. A moment later she heard a car pass. Then he moved out of sight.

She stood trembling, waiting for him to reappear. Seconds ticked by, and finally she saw him, trotting back to her.

"They wiped away the trail of the van. You could miss it easily," he said.

"What marker did you leave?" she asked.

"Five flat stones, stacked one on the other."

"Like a trail marker?"

"Yes."

Carter led them a short distance from the van and left more marks, though these he scratched in the dirt. She recognized them as Native symbols but did not know the meaning.

He drew a crooked arrow and a bull's eye, and what looked like a butterfly and then several wagon wheels.

"What does that mean?" she asked.

He pointed at the crooked arrow first and then moved from one symbol to the next.

"This one is Lightning Snake. It means escape. It will tell them we made it out. This is Buffalo Eye and signifies the need for alertness. I hope they will read that our attackers are still out there. This is a saddlebag."

"I thought it was a butterfly."

He smiled. "Saddlebags mean a journey. It will tell them that we are traveling, and this means Hogans," he said referring to the pictorial representation of the traditional domed dwelling of their people. "To let them know that we are traveling toward a town."

"Which town? Phoenix or home?" she asked.

He drew one more symbol, a series of connected straight lines and one wavy one.

"Water," she said.

Then he made a vertical line and the water symbol. He repeated this once more.

"Water. Dam. Water. Dam," he said, pointing.

"Mesa Salado Dam, Antelope Lake, Red Rock Dam, Turquoise Lake, Hogan. Home at Turquoise Reservation."

He nodded and gave her a smile.

"You said your younger brother Tommy was a Shadow Wolf. He reads sign."

"Yes. And Jack, Ray and Dylan were marines. But more importantly we are Apache. They'll know where to find us."

She studied his work, hoping their people would find them quickly.

"Anything else?" he asked.

"Why did you kiss me?"

His smile broadened. "That answer might take longer."

He offered her the water bottle, and she took another swallow. Many rough miles lay between them and civilization. It was only February and approaching noon, and the temperature felt well into the eighties. And the dry heat of the desert was already stealing away their strength.

Carter motioned back to the dry wash. They picked their way carefully now, conserving energy and stopping at mid-afternoon when the sun had dipped enough to allow the wall of the wash to cast enough shade to sit in. They had the rest of the first bottle of water and ate the pretzels he had commandeered from the FBI's stash.

The salt tasted so good she licked her fingers, and when she finished she found him watching her again.

The lowered lids and the intent stare both made her stomach flutter and her body come to tingling awareness.

"What?" she asked.

"You're beautiful," he said.

She flushed.

"And you can run like the wind."

"Same goes for you," she said, now letting her attention wander over the thirsty sand and wilted gray-green trees that hugged the banks waiting for rain.

"I hate it down here in the flats," she admitted.

He nodded, understanding that. "We belong in the mountains."

"I keep seeing their faces. All the ones I worked with."

He wrapped an arm about her.

"They'll be burying them soon," she said. "This weekend, I'll bet. And I won't be there."

"At least you won't be buried with them."

Her gaze flashed to his. Then she rested her head on his shoulder, not knowing if she should feel lucky or cursed.

"I'd do anything to catch that guy," she said. "See that he goes to prison for the rest of his life."

He gave her a squeeze. "I've been thinking about what you said back there, about him working with law enforcement. I'm afraid it makes a lot of sense."

She sighed and snuggled closer.

"And, Amber? I haven't seen anyone seriously since you left. Now I know why. I still want you."

She tensed and lifted her head. "Carter, we've been apart a long time."

"Are you seeing someone?"

"No," she admitted. "Just afraid."

He blew out a breath.

"What is it you are afraid of, Amber?"

"Besides dying?" she chuckled. "I don't want to be like my parents."

"And what do you want?"

She sighed. "What I can't have. To live near my sisters, watch my nephews grow up." Be Turquoise Mountain Apache, she thought.

He noted that none of her ambitions involved changing her identity. He also noticed she did not say she wanted him.

"I wished you had come to me. Confided what he did."

"You were in basic when I figured it all out."

He stopped walking and turned to her. "Amber, you talk about trust. But you didn't trust me to help you. You didn't come to me for help when you needed it. How do you think that makes me feel?"

"You were gone, Carter. I was there alone."

"You chose to handle it alone. I would have helped you. I'd like someone who believes in me enough to stick around, even when I don't understand."

She dragged her toe in the sand, making an arching line. "I was afraid."

"Of me?"

"Of being trapped."

"Is that how you see our marriage?"

"At the time I did. You said I was my parents' responsibility and then I would be yours. I don't want to be passed along like a child, Carter. I want a partner, not a keeper."

"I was eighteen, Amber. I was trying to be a man. Take care of things. Take care of you."

"I know."

"I can't stop thinking of it and of us. I keep wondering if it could work between us."

"Carter, we almost died again today. It's natural to want to grab a hold of someone."

"Not someone. You."

She lifted a hand in the direction they had been heading, calling an end to the rest. "We should get moving."

"Amber."

"Not now, Carter. Please."

"When? They came after us again. If you hadn't recognized that guy, we might be dead right now. So I'm wondering, Amber, when is the right time to talk about the things that really matter? Things like how you smell and how you taste. And how much I want to make love to you again."

"I don't."

"What do you want, Amber?"

She looked around with frantic eyes. "I just want to get out of this arroyo."

"Back to Turquoise Canyon," he said.

She rounded on him, fists tight at her side. "That's never going to happen, Carter! Not for me. You can go back there and you should. But I can't."

Was she trying to protect him?

He slapped himself in the forehead as he remembered what Jack had told him and given him.

She gave him an odd look.

"You don't want me to lose the tribe, my brothers, Tribal Thunder."

"Who?"

"That's our name. Me, Ray, Dylan and Jack. Kenshaw calls us Tribal Thunder."

"Carter, what are you talking about?"

"You, protecting me. Keeping me with the tribe."

"Well, of course. You love Turquoise Canyon. It's your home. I don't want you to lose it because of me."

He explained that because she had been a minor at the time she was withdrawn from the enrollment by her parent, as an adult, she could now reapply.

Her eyes widened. "Is that possible?"

"Yes." Carter dipped to a knee and retrieved the correct papers from his duffel. Then he stood and offered them to her. "Application to reinstate."

Her face lit up, and her smile dazzled. "I could. Are you sure?"

He nodded. Instead of taking the papers, Amber threw herself into his arms, and her words were muffled against his shoulder, but he understood her.

"I could come home."

But not if the US Marshals had anything to say about it.

Chapter Eighteen

The sun's low angle painted the landscape pink as they walked wearily along.

Carter's words buzzed in her mind as they trod south. She could rejoin the tribe. She could right the wrong her father had done her. She had already filled out the application that Carter again carried in his bag. She would give it to the tribe as soon as they reached home.

If they reached home.

Their destination, the Saguaro Flats tribe, was an even smaller Native American community than Turquoise Canyon, also of the Tonto band, who lived in a reservation on the outskirts of Phoenix since winning a lawsuit against the US government in the 1970s.

Carter paused. "Listen."

Car doors slammed, and voices murmured. They crept to the edge of the wash. She peered over the lip of the bank but could see nothing past the vegetation.

Together they crawled up to ground level and peeked through the juniper brush at an isolated gas station.

"What should we do?" she asked.

There was a battered blue pickup truck at the pumps but no driver. A few minutes later two men emerged from the convenience store and strode toward the truck. One tapped a pack of cigarettes as he climbed behind the wheel and set them in motion.

"We need a ride," she said. "They left it open with the keys inside."

"You want to steal a vehicle?" he asked.

"Yes."

"Okay." Carter scouted the area. "Good cover on the west side by the dumpster. You wait here."

"The hell I will."

He scowled at her but didn't ask her to remain behind again. Instead he took both guns from the duffel.

"You know how to shoot one of these?" he asked.

She wrinkled her nose and shook her head.

He blew away a breath and shoved one gun in his front pocket and the second in the waistband of his jeans.

"Tuck in your braid," Amber said.

"What?"

"They're searching for us. Two Apache Indians."

He gave her a look as if to say this was not going to substantially change his appearance, but his braid did get tucked under the collar of his dirty oxford shirt.

They had to cross the highway to reach cover. The gas station was painted in earth tones like the red rock hills beyond. The green dumpster lay far to the left past the large red, white and blue sun shield above the four pumps. To the right lay a three-car garage with all bays shut. Two cars were parked between the dumpster and the side of the squatty building.

The entire journey was only a quarter mile but took them almost an hour because of the need to move without notice. And another twenty minutes because of one failed attempt to find a driver who left his vehicle unlocked with the keys in the ignition.

It was dusk when a spotless gray compact pulled in.

"See the white sticker with the bar code on the windshield?" he asked. "That means that is a rental."

She glanced at the decal as the driver stepped out from behind the wheel and stretched. He fumbled around in the compartment opening the trunk lock before releasing the latch to the gas tank, then filled up. When he left the car for the convenience store, Amber followed as far as the front window. There she scouted the driver.

"Buying beer," she said.

Carter walked past the pumps, glanced inside and spotted the keys. He nodded at Amber who walked quickly to the passenger side of the car. Carter closed the trunk and slipped into the driver's seat. They were away a moment later.

"He'll call the cops and they'll notify the Feds. We might have a ten minute head start," said Carter.

"Saguaro Flats Indian Reservation is fifteen miles away."

He gripped the wheel as his foot pressed the gas. "I know."

"Are we going to stop at Saguaro?" she asked.

"I'd feel better in Turquoise Canyon."

"Long way to go in a stolen car," she said.

He nodded his agreement and gripped the wheel. "Let's get on Indian Land."

Amber glanced at the digital clock on the dash and wondered if the driver had noticed the theft yet. She looked behind them for headlights.

Carter's gaze flicked to the rearview. "See anything?" he asked.

"Not yet."

But they were coming. The bad guys and the good guys. And she knew that they would not be able to tell the difference.

"How long?" she asked.

"If they are near where we started, they'll be on us anytime."

"Do you think we should leave this car and get another?"

"Where?"

She shook her head, bewildered. There was nothing out here but the desert and the sky and the hum of the tires.

"Headlights," he said.

"What if it's the police? We can't start shooting. They might be the real police," she said.

"Closing," he said, his gaze flashing from the rearview mirror and then back to her.

They were still off the Saguaro Flats Indian Reservation property.

The lights in the grille of the car behind them flashed blue and red.

"Unmarked car," she said, glancing back. "State police?"

He pursed his lips. "Don't know."

"You stopping?"

"If I do, I might have to shoot someone."

"You can't outrun them."

"Honest cop won't shoot at us or try to run us off the road. Let's see what he does."

The answer came a moment later when the car rammed them from behind. The jolt engaged her safety belt, the nylon gripping her shoulder as they careened into the opposite side of the two-lane highway.

"We won't make it," she said.

The pursuing vehicle drew beside them and bumped Amber's door. She turned toward the new threat and got a very good look at the driver. She gave a little shout and lifted a finger to point at him. His eyes widened and the driver tugged the wheel, separating their vehicles.

"How many?" Carter asked.

"One."

"You recognize him?" Carter asked.

"Yes. The...the guy. The fake FBI guy."

"What guy?"

"Driving the Subaru. The one with the busted nose. Leopold."

Carter set his jaw. "Hold on."

Carter turned the wheel, and this time he hit the other car. The impact jarred her, and the sound of squealing metal filled the air. The two vehicles raced parallel for a moment and then drifted toward the shoulder. Carter kept turning the wheel, forcing the unmarked vehicle over. When the car's wheels left the pavement, the other vehicle jolted, swerved and they flew on.

Amber released a held breath a moment before their back windshield shattered.

"Get down," Carter said, hunching as he drove.

Amber ducked, but there was no second shot.

"This is so bad," she said.

They drove in silence, the warm dry wind swirling through the gap in the rear window.

"Do you see him?" she asked.

"No." Carter kept both hands on the wheel, but hunched now as if someone had hit him in the stomach.

"Was that a shotgun?" she asked, checking the damaged window, surveying the fist-sized hole and the rear seat glittering with cubes of glass.

"Pistol. Lucky shot."

Amber blinked at the hole, wondering where the bullet went. She had her answer a moment later when she looked at Carter and saw a dark stain welling on the white fabric at the top of his right shoulder.

"You're bleeding!"

"Yeah."

"Yeah? That's it, just yeah?" Her voice held a frightening note of panic. What would she do if he was seriously injured? How would she get them to safety?

"How bad?" she asked.

"Don't know. Burns like a mother…" His words trailed off.

She unfastened her belt and reached, then hesitated. There was a hole in the top of his shirt. She placed her right and left index finger in the gap and tugged, rending the fabric.

He sucked in a breath between his teeth, the sound a hiss.

She could see his skin now, orange in the dashboard light. The rounded muscle of his shoulder was marred by a black groove from which blood welled at an alarming rate and ran down his skin in crimson rivers.

"Aw!" Carter cried. "Right though the medicine shield."

The bullet had grazed the skin at his shoulder, cutting a channel through the top of his bear track tattoo.

"What's in that bag? Do you have a shirt or something?" she asked.

"Yes."

She scrambled to get something to stop the bleeding and came up with a soft cotton T-shirt which she folded into a pad and pressed to his shoulder. He dipped away from her touch and winced.

"Damn, that hurts."

"Seems like it grazed the skin." She continued to press down. Before them a green-and-white sign announced the Saguaro Flats Indian Reservation.

"We're on reservation land."

"Is he back there?"

"Not yet."

He pulled into the visitor's center, closed now and without anyone in the parking lot. Carter drove behind the square building that was little more than a trailer on blocks.

Here he turned off both headlights and motor.

They had a clear view of the road. It was not more than a minute later the unmarked car flew past them, with its one functioning headlight.

"We have to lose this car."

Amber insisted that they dress his wound before moving. He held the sodden T-shirt as she tore up a second one. She wrapped it around his chest and shoulder, trying not to react to the nearness of him and failing as usual.

"What?" he asked.

"I just can't seem to touch you without…"

He lifted his brow and grinned.

"You just got shot," she said, her voice disapproving.

"But I'm not dead." He laughed and kissed her hard.

For just a moment she forgot where she was and why this was such a bad idea. His tongue grazed hers, and she opened for him. He deepened the kiss, his mouth slanting across hers, their tongues lapping and sliding against one another. She lifted her hand to hold him and touched the bandage. Amber pulled back.

He smiled at her, his face now blue under the starlight.

Carter twisted the key, and the engine hummed. He left the lights off as he drove, stopping at a house that had a barn beside it and several trucks in various states of repair. Carter pulled into the grouping of vehicles and left her to investigate. All the trucks had the keys dangling from their ignitions. He took the first one that turned over, leaving the rental with the rest promising himself to get the truck back to the owner when possible. It was safer that whoever lived in that house knew nothing about them. Less than an hour later they were on the road leading to Kurt's home. Carter pulled over well before the drive because he wanted to scout the place first to be certain they were alone and he didn't want the stolen truck at Kurt's place.

"More walking," he said and reached for the door.

She followed him out, insisting on carrying his bag.

"How far to your brother's place?" she asked.

"A mile or two."

"Why Kurt's place?" she asked.

"Kurt lives at the fire station as much as home, and he lives alone. Plus, he can get a message to Jack."

"They might be watching there, too."

"I'll make sure we're alone."

She felt her insides heat at that thought and admonished herself. The man had a bullet wound. But still images of Carter running shirtless down the arroyo filled her mind and her fantasies.

They opted to walk well off the shoulder of the road and the reach of the headlights of passing cars. The road was sparsely populated with residences, including the concrete block ranch belonging to his youngest brother. The empty carport and dark windows told them Kurt was out.

"Looking for us again, I'll bet," he said.

They watched the house for some time, and Carter scouted the perimeter. She watched him, a moving shadow creeping past the basketball hoop rising from a flat concrete slab beside a small shed. He moved silently under the carport, past the barbecue grill and then disappeared.

She held her breath, released it and then held it again. On the third breath he reappeared and waved her over. She joined him in the driveway at the side entrance.

She smiled. Her feet ached and her body ached, and she had never been more thirsty in her life.

He put a hand on the knob.

"It's not locked?" she asked.

Carter glanced back over his shoulder. "Kurt has an alarm system."

That surprised her. No one she knew had an alarm system.

"Wait here a minute."

Amber held her breath. Had the men who were after them anticipated Carter's move?

She wanted to call him back, suddenly afraid they were waiting for him in there.

Then she saw something inside move past the window.

"Carter wait," she whispered.

But he was already turning the knob and stepping into the house.

Chapter Nineteen

Carter's entrance set off a wild barking from Kurt's large dog. He had been to the house when Kurt was not here, and he knew that his dog, Justice, did not like visitors when his master was away. Carter had fed him when Kurt was away at school, but he had never brought another person into the house. If he had to, he'd chain the dog outside.

He paused in the kitchen as the dog continued his frantic barking. The room was illuminated by the small hood lamp over the stove. But the living room beyond was dark.

"Justice!" he said in his sternest voice. "Quiet."

The dog went silent and approached from the darkness.

Carter knew the dog could see much better than he could in the low light. All he could make out was a moving shadow and the bulk of the huge head of the pit bull.

The dog was halfway across the kitchen before Carter saw the tail wagging. He relaxed his shoulders. The dog paused and sniffed. Carter didn't know if he picked up the scent of blood or of the other human, but his hackles lifted, and he began to growl.

Carter took a chance and flicked on the light. Then he lowered himself to one knee and held out his hand.

"Damn it, Justice. You know me."

Justice pinned his beady eyes on Carter and finally the tail twitched.

"Carter?" came the whisper from behind him. "Someone is coming. A car."

He flipped off the light and drew her inside. Justice growled again.

"Quiet," he said. The dog weighed at least seventy pounds and had all his working parts.

Carter kept Amber behind him as he pulled her through the kitchen to the window over the sink. Together they watched the car roll slowly past and out of sight.

"Do you think it was him?"

"Not the same car," he answered. But he knew there was more than one man after them. He turned to find Justice halfway across the kitchen, sniffing. "Justice, I swear I will shoot you."

"He's big," she said.

"You like dogs?"

"I like cats."

Carter spoke to the dog in Apache. He told Justice that Amber was a friend and a beautiful woman and that she was welcome in his brother's house.

"That dog speaks Tonto Apache?" she asked.

"I hope so."

Finally the tail began to move, and Carter put out his hand again. Amber slowly offered hers, and Justice poked her with his wet black nose. Then he sniffed her leg and finally stuck his nose in her crotch.

Carter pulled him off. "Enough of that."

Justice sat, and Carter fed him a bowl full of chow with water. While the dog inhaled his food, Carter went to the refrigerator and retrieved two bottles of cold water. They drank them dry and then had two more.

"How are you feeling?" he asked.

She had a dull headache, and she was tired to the bone. But she was not the one who had been shot.

"We need to get you cleaned up. Does Kurt have a first aid kit?"

"He's a paramedic, so he better."

"Should you call your brother?" she asked.

"Kurt doesn't have a landline. Just uses his cell."

"What about your phone?"

"I don't trust it."

"When will he be home?"

Carter shrugged and then winced.

"Your family will be worried," she said.

"Yours, too."

They stared in silence a moment. She thought of her application to come home. Where would she live? Her thoughts turned to Carter, and the desire sparked in her chest, flooding downward to ignite her longing, deep, low and hot.

"Let's get a bandage on that."

They headed for the bathroom in the back of the house and flicked on the light. Amber found a shoe box with some medical supplies, including large gauze pads and antiseptic cream. Amber seated Carter on the edge of the tub and helped him remove the improvised bandage and his ruined shirt. The wound had begun to clot, but the removal of the dressing caused it to bleed again, sending a scarlet trail of blood down his arm. He scowled at his shoulder as if it disappointed him.

"It doesn't look too bad," she lied, when in fact, it looked terrible. The edges of the wound were raw and angry red. The inside of the groove looked like raw meat, and the entire thing made her stomach roll.

"You ever cleaned a wound before?"

"Of course." She rubbed her mouth and recalled the lip that she had iced but not had stitched until the next day because no one had noticed it until then.

Justice entered the room and sat nearly on Amber's foot as she washed her hands with soap, relishing the feel of clean skin. Then she filled the sink with soapy water and set to work with a washcloth, washing away the blood. She tried not to admire the firm bronze skin beneath the cloth or the feel of his muscles where she gripped his arm. But she could not ignore the tiny white scars, divots and puckers that marred the skin of his arm. The marks left by the shrapnel and the surgeries to remove the tiny bits of metal.

"Do these hurt?" she asked.

"Not too much. The scar tissue tugs, and I have some numb places."

"Here?" she asked, moving the cloth in a rhythmic motion.

"No," his voice was lower now, gruff. "I can feel all that."

She continued working from his wrist and spiraling up, pausing only to rinse off the blood. One stubborn line of blood continued to flow like a river down the bright ink of his tattoo and the wide plain of his chest muscles to settle in his ribbed stomach.

She washed his stomach and chest, feeling his gaze fixed on her and refusing to look. His nipple pebbled at the touch of the cloth, and she wondered what it would be like to stroke him again and feel his body come alive. His chest rose and fell a little too fast.

He wanted to make love to her. He had told her so.

Amber lifted her gaze and found fathomless brown eyes, parted lips and an expression that registered as a different sort of pain, one tied to the same longing that thumped in her chest.

He reached his good hand out and captured her around the neck, pulling her down to kiss him again. She sank between his splayed knees and let the sensations flow. Her body stirred, and the cloth fell from her hands.

A cold nose poked her in the center of her back.

She yelped and turned. Justice sat with tongue lolling and eyes half closed.

"Justice," growled Carter. "Lie down."

The dog whined and made a show of lying down but then decided to sit on the bath mat instead.

"Let me finish up," she said, lifting the cloth and ringing it out once more. The trail of blood was back, but this time she elected to smear a piece of gauze with antiseptic gel before placing it over the open wound. "That really needs a stitch or two."

"Not going to happen."

"It will scar."

"Make me look even tougher," he said and prodded at the gauze.

She added several more pieces until the blood no longer soaked through. Then she used a two-inch ACE bandage to hold it in place. When she finished, the bandage wove around his chest, under his armpit and back around his arm in a figure eight.

"Nice. Where'd you learn that?"

"I had a rotator cuff strain. That's how we held the ice bag in place."

He nodded. She used the washcloth once more to clean away the last trail of blood.

"Eating or washing next?" he asked.

She was too tired for either, but she suggested he take a bath so he didn't soak his wound, and she offered to find them something to eat.

"I don't know what he has. Might be slim pickings."

She left him, anxious to be away from the need he stirred and the bad ideas that kept popping up. What if they were caught and killed? Would she want to spend her last hours on this earth avoiding Carter or in his arms?

She knew the answer, and that frightened her in an entirely different way. Under normal circumstances, she would use her head. But nothing about this was normal.

She heard the bath water running as she made it to the kitchen. She didn't dare turn on the light, so she worked in the near dark. The freezer had one bag of pinto beans, ice and frozen burritos.

But in the refrigerator, she struck gold. Onions, potatoes, eggs and a nice defrosted steak. The sound of the water stream stopped, only to be replaced by splashing and humming. She focused on the cast-iron skillet and scrambling eggs. She was not imagining Carter naked and wet in the bathtub. She was not picturing all that bronze wet skin, those long muscular legs and that tight ass.

Amber groaned as she chopped the potatoes thinly so they'd cook faster. She was hungry enough to eat them raw. She had done this job often enough to be able to do it in the dark. Her first job had been off the books in the kitchen of a diner in Darabee. Into the hot pan went grease, the onions and potatoes. She added salt, pepper, paprika and cayenne for the frying potatoes.

By the time the bathroom door opened, she had the steak seasoned.

Carter emerged, wearing clean jeans, a white T-shirt, bare feet and a devilish grin.

"Smells like heaven."

"It will be a few minutes for the potatoes," she said. "You go shower. I'll do this."

She lifted her eyebrows. A man who could cook was a thing of beauty.

"I opted to leave the overhead light off. But I kept that one on."

"Fine. Go get cleaned up." He lifted a meat fork from the container of utensils beside the stove and poked at a potato. Amber moved aside.

She hesitated because she did not have the bag Kay had packed.

"Would your brother mind if I borrowed something to wear?"

"I already put out a T-shirt and a pair of pajama bottoms I know he has never worn."

"How do you know that?"

"Because he sleeps naked, like me." His brow lifted, and she felt the flush rising up her neck and heating her face.

She nodded and backed away.

"I put them in the bathroom. See you in a few."

Amber retreated to the bathroom and closed the door behind her, leaning back against the wood and releasing a breath. That man made her hotter than those frying potatoes.

She stripped out of the dirty clothes, keeping nothing but the necklace, and the bra and panties that she rinsed out in the sink and hung to dry.

Then she started the taps and stepped into the warm stream. There were few things that could not be made better by a hot shower. Amber emerged a few minutes later and tried to ignore the sensitivity of her skin as she toweled herself dry.

She was going to eat and sleep and pray that the next time she saw any law enforcement, they would be wearing the seal of the Turquoise Canyon Tribal Police.

She wondered if Carter was now imagining her damp and naked. A smile curled her lips. Then she shook her head at her reflection. She was not going to let her lust overcome her common sense. She was tired and frightened. He was safe and familiar. That was all.

Her reflection gave her a look of skepticism, and she groaned, turning away.

He wasn't just safe and familiar. He was her first true love, and those feelings died hard.

Amber tugged on the fleece pajama bottoms and frowned. They were covered with images of playing cards, poker chips and arrowheads. Clearly they were from the tribe's casino, and she could see why a man would not want to wear them. But they were clean, and so was the soft red T-shirt.

She entered the kitchen to the sound of the steak sizzling in the pan. The aroma made her stomach rumble. She closed her eyes and inhaled.

"Wow."

He smiled at her, spatula in one hand as his gaze

swept her from head to heel. "You even make that look good." He pointed the spatula at the small dinette and said, "Sit."

Justice was already sleeping under the table, so she was careful with her chair. He lifted his head and then laid it back down.

"He's not going to beg?" she asked.

"Kurt never feeds him from the table. He gets leftovers in his dish with breakfast. If there are any. I'm hungry enough to eat that dog."

Justice sighed but did not rouse again as Carter brought her a plate. He'd added toast to her original menu, and she slathered the offering with butter and dug in.

He added ketchup to his eggs, and they both finished another full glass of water. Her headache was easing, and she wondered if it had to do with dehydration, fatigue or famine.

There was no conversation as they ate, and, as Carter predicted, there was little but gristle and a small portion of eggs left for Justice.

"I wish you could get word to your brother," she said. "I'm sure he's worried sick."

"They'll be on our trail. Likely made it to the gas station by now.

"No helping it. He'll be back sometime. Tonight. Tomorrow. I'll see him then."

She wondered if Kurt would take the forms to the tribal council for her. She rested her cheek on her hand and sagged. "What now?"

Her eyes blinked, and she had trouble keeping them

open. Amazing what clean clothes and a full stomach could do.

"Come on, Sleeping Beauty. Let's get you to bed."

Amber suddenly did not feel sleepy anymore.

Chapter Twenty

Carter watched Amber's eyes go from that sexy heavy-lidded stare to wide-eyed. He wanted to take her to his bed, but she had looked dead on her feet. Now her stare looked hungry.

"Put you to bed," he said. "Not take you to bed."

Her shoulders sank a fraction. Was that disappointment he read in her expression? He wondered about old mistakes. His. Hers. Then he thought about new beginnings. If anyone deserved happiness, it was Amber. Could he be the one to bring her life joy and meaning?

"Kurt has two bedrooms. His and one that Thomas uses when he is back from the Shadow Wolves. But I'll bet he's tracking us right now."

"Sad. Here we are in their home, and they are out there searching for us.

"Can't be helped."

"When will Kurt be back?"

"Not sure but definitely by morning, because he didn't take Justice along. Come on." He took their dishes to the sink and dropped them. She glanced at the dirty frying pan. "Leave it. Just more tracks for them to follow."

He clasped her hand and led her to Thomas's room.

"This is it."

There was little but a full-sized bed, side table and a bench along the window.

She stood in the door peeking in. "Where will you be?"

He moved to the door, and she stepped back but not enough, and their bodies grazed as he passed by. He stilled and looked down at her.

"You want to see where I'll be sleeping?" he asked.

She nodded.

He led her across the hall to Kurt's room. The bed was larger, and the furnishing included a desk and computer setup.

"Room for two," she said.

He turned to her. "Like last night?"

She shook her head. "No. Like before I left."

He watched her expression for clues. Why now? he wondered. Was it because she had hope now, hope of return to her tribe, her family and him?

"I just need you tonight."

Now why did it bother him that she said tonight? He knew why. It implied that she wouldn't need him every night or any night or all nights from here to eternity. *Just tonight.*

He should take what she offered with both hands. Instead he hesitated because he wanted more, a promise, a commitment and second chance. What did she want?

"Need the bathroom?" he asked.

She nodded and retreated there. Carter dived over the bed and opened Kurt's side table, praying aloud. He found what he was looking for, condoms of the bare skin variety. And something else, a little red squishy packet of something unfamiliar. The packet read, *Pleasure-enhancing lubricant.*

Holy heck. Now he needed to change the sheets. Where were the clean sheets? Hall closet. Inside the bathroom the water ran. He stripped the bed and made it fresh in record time. Amber emerged to find him throwing the coverlet back in place.

"You changed the sheets?" There was joy and wonder in her voice.

He nodded.

"That's sexy as hell."

He grinned. She lifted the two foil packages and considered them as his body went hot. She lowered the lubricant to the side table.

"Won't need this," she said, her eyes flashing to him.

Was she already wet for him? His skin went hot, and then he shivered with anticipation.

She raised the condom. "Might need more of these."

"I'll be right back." He hit the bathroom, finding a bottle of ibuprofen and taking three. His shoulder throbbed dully, but he knew Amber would make him forget all about it. The throbbing moved south.

When he came back, he found her curled up under the coverlet, her eyes closed and her breathing soft and even.

He stood there staring at her as his disappointment gradually turned to a twisting feeling in his stomach. The disappointment tugged, but as he gazed down at the small bump under the coverlet he began to see how little she was and feel the need to keep her safe pulling at his heart. Carter rubbed a hand over his chest trying to ease the aching there. It didn't.

Carter wanted to protect her, of course. Not just now but always. He was falling again. He knew it, and it scared him. How had he found the courage before—to offer that ring and take her into his heart, knowing she might not stay?

AMBER ROUSED IN the stillness of the night. She lay on her side tucked up close to Carter's warm body. Her leg was bent and resting on his muscular thigh, her head nestled on his good shoulder and his arm wrapped protectively around her back. His breath was slow and easy, but something had awakened her. She lifted her head from the pillow to listen. She caught movement, thinking it looked like a man crouched at the foot of the bed.

Her heart slammed into her chest as she sat up. Carter followed, his body swayed, and he groaned.

"What?" he asked.

One furry paw lifted to the end of the mattress, followed by another. Then the massive head of the pit bull lifted in silhouette against the curtains and the moonlight beyond.

"Justice!" said Carter. "Off the bed."

Justice paused and then continued his slow crawl forward.

Carter raked a hand through his hair and turned to Amber. "Kurt lets him sleep in his bed."

He threw back the covers and sat on the edge of the mattress, pointing toward the hall as he ordered Justice from the bedroom. Then he closed the door before returning to her.

"Sorry about that."

"He scared the life out of me. For a minute I thought someone was in the room."

"He's a good dog. Friendly with kids and most other dogs. The female dogs."

She giggled. "Like Kurt."

He lay back and pulled her down beside her.

"How's the shoulder?" she asked.

"It burns."

"Will you be able to sleep again?"

He turned his head and gazed at her, his dark eyes black in the night. He lifted a finger and traced the outline of the scar at her mouth, and then he traced the outline of her lower lip. She trembled as the tingling awareness rolled through her body with the power of a flash flood. She rested a hand on his chest, feeling the rapid heartbeat that matched her own.

"You want to?" he asked.

She nodded. "But I don't want to hurt your shoulder."

"We can go slow." His smile was filled with male sensuality. Somehow he made her ache down low and deep without even touching her.

She tried to remember why this was such a bad idea. Their first time she had been young, giddy and nervous. Now she was lonely and scared. She wanted comfort more than sex, didn't she?

Nope. She wanted sex with Carter Bear Den. Throbbing and raw. She wanted to feel him sliding in and out of her body, and she wanted to press herself up close and tight. Tomorrow his brother would come, and she would be in protective custody again. Tonight she wanted only to be in Carter's custody. So she could take what he offered.

Amber raked her fingers over the hard muscle of his chest, and Carter's eyes widened, flashing with heat.

He dragged her against him, as if she weighed nothing at all. As if he had not been shot tonight. As if she were the most important thing in the world to him.

Carter was very good in bed. Too good. She remembered that as he kissed her. But in the blending of lips and the fierce thrusting of tongues, she forgot everything but him.

Chapter Twenty-One

Carter breathed in the sweet smell of her clean hair. Brushing it back, he exhaled upon her exposed neck and felt her tremble. Her long hair and onyx eyes captivated him. He stared at her beautiful face and then ran his hand from her shoulder to her hip.

He'd had women since Amber. But they'd all been a poor substitute. He admitted that now, but only to himself. He hadn't moved on. Not even close. How could he when he still loved her? Every frustrating, beautiful, intoxicating inch of her.

He measured the span of her hips with his splayed hands. She had the wide, full hips of a woman, and the narrow waist of a girl. His desire for her grew with an anticipation that he understood was more than physical. He wanted to please her, of course, but also, at some primal level, he wanted to make her his again.

Amber lifted up so that she straddled his hips.

"You want top?" he asked.

"Keep you from bleeding all over the sheets," she said, her smile sweet. "Are you sure you're—"

"I'm fine."

She lay on top of him, her knees bent at his sides and her body still. He didn't know if she was being sure he was well enough for this or reconsidering. Gradually she slid her hips over his so that he throbbed beneath her. It was hard not to move.

"Still okay?"

"Amber, you don't need to keep checking. I'll tell you if it hurts."

"Does it?"

"In all the right places." He lifted his hips, and her eyes widened as he slid against her.

A sensual smile curled her lips.

He took a long look at Amber in the near darkness, knowing he needed to keep this picture for always. Her skin glowed blue as moonlight on snow, and her smile welcomed him.

He lifted his hands to her waist and stared at that flat stomach. His thumbs rubbed back and forth over taut skin as he wondered what it would be like to make a family with Amber.

He stilled, and his hands dropped away from her.

"Carter?" She dipped down to rest on her elbows to look at him, her full bare breasts now hanging just an inch above his chest.

He dragged a hand slowly along the center of her back and then pushed her forward so she fell on to his chest. Her body trembled with awareness and need as he stroked her thigh. Amber savored the tingling sensation of his fingers gliding slowly over her.

He pressed her tight against his naked chest and kissed her deeply as he pushed inside her.

They were better than before, and she nearly cried with joy at this reunion.

When they were both sated, breathing heavily, their hearts still thudding, they came to rest.

"I missed this. Missed you," he whispered and kissed her temple.

"Me, too. That was wonderful."

He made a humming sound of agreement. Her eyes drifted closed. Her body still buzzed with pleasure. She blinked her eyes, trying to think.

"Are you all right?" she whispered.

"Never better." His words had that tired slur of a man not really awake, falling as she was, into slumber.

He brushed a stray lock of hair away from her face, his hand unusually clumsy. She pressed her lips to his neck and then closed her eyes, still draped across him like a second blanket.

She did not know how long she slept, but when she next opened her eyes it was to the barking of a large dog.

Carter was out of bed in an instant. Morning light flooded around the cracks of the curtains.

"Who is it?" she said.

"Stay here."

He tugged on a pair of athletic shorts and retrieved one of the pistols from his duffel.

She lifted the sheets to her chest and then realized how ridiculous that was as a means of protection, so she scrambled from the other side of the bed. She shimmied into the polar fleece bottoms and dived into the red T-shirt. Carter had already vanished down the hall.

Justice had stopped barking. Amber stilled. Did he know the intruder or had someone silenced the dog?

CARTER STOOD FLATTENED against the wall between the kitchen and living room listening to the car door slam.

A moment later, the front door opened. Justice continued to bark, but the inflection was different.

Carter suspected it was Kurt, but he waited until he heard his brother greet his dog and then let him out in the yard.

"Kurt?" Carter called. "It's Carter."

"Carter?" came the reply, his brother's voice full of shock.

"Coming in," he said.

When Carter stepped into the kitchen a moment later it was to find his brother standing beside the sink of dirty dishes with his gun drawn. Carter held up his good hand with the pistol. The other arm just didn't cooperate, so he left it half-raised.

Kurt looked like hell. Red eyes, dust covering his jeans and jacket. But instead of yelling at Carter for worrying them, his kid brother grabbed Carter in a bear hug.

The embrace hurt Carter, and he didn't quite keep the groan from escaping.

"What happened?" asked Kurt. "You okay? Mom's worried sick and Jack…" He blew out a breath and put Carter at arm's length.

Carter glanced toward the bedroom as Kurt followed the direction of his gaze.

"Amber? It's Kurt. Come out."

She stepped from Kurt's bedroom door and into the hall on slender bare feet. The dragging hems of the fleece bottoms had been rolled, but the over large T-shirt did not hide that she wore nothing beneath. Carter looked to Kurt, whose eyes widened at the picture she made, her hair still tangled from sleep and her eyes half-lidded.

Carter tucked the pistol in the pocket of his shorts.

Kurt's eyes widened even more, and he made a humming sound before glancing away.

"We've been looking for you two."

When Kurt turned back to his brother, Carter found his cheeks a little too pink and his voice a little too breathless.

"What happened to you?" Kurt said, finally noticing the ACE bandage still holding the dressing in place.

"Got shot."

Kurt's bright smile dropped away. "Shot?"

"Last night," said Amber.

"Let me check it."

"Call Jack first," Carter said.

Kurt reached for his phone. Carter stayed his hand.

"No cell phones."

Kurt blinked at him. "That's all I have. Wait, you want me to leave?"

Carter nodded.

"After I check that."

"All right."

Carter sat on a kitchen chair as Kurt unwrapped the bandage and peered beneath the dressing.

"Needs a stitch or two."

"So, stitch it."

Kurt worked as a paramedic, mostly in the air ambulance flying folks from rural areas to the larger medical facilities in Phoenix. His brother kept his personal medical kit in his truck and a similar collection of supplies in his home.

A few minutes later Carter was regretting his words, but Kurt was quick and competent. He added antibiotics to the treatment and had Carter's throbbing, stitched, disinfected shoulder dressed and bandaged again.

FROM OUTSIDE THE DOOR, Justice scratched and whined. Amber stepped toward the door, and Carter grabbed her hand.

"Let Kurt do it."

She understood. He didn't want her seen from the drive. Kurt let his dog inside. Justice was all wiggles and whines for the three of them until Kurt gave him his breakfast, and he settled down.

"You want to fill me in or should I go first?" asked Kurt.

"You first," said Carter.

Amber sat at the kitchen table, leaving the opposite chair vacant. Kurt drew a water bottle from the refrigerator, while Carter leaned against the counter nearby.

They looked a lot alike, she realized. Same soft brown eyes and black hair. Similar bronze skin color, though it looked like Kurt spent more time outdoors. They were close in height and body build and the wide set of their eyes. But Kurt's face was younger, less angular, and his eyes held an openness missing from Carter's. Their similar build and appearance only highlighted to her more vividly how different their brother Jack was by comparison.

"Well, I heard on the news that the mine admitted that some supplies are unaccounted for. News speculations that we're talking explosives."

"What did the authorities say?" asked Amber.

"What they always say. 'No comment.'"

Amber's stomach squeezed at this. Why hadn't she

suspected wrongdoing instead of chalking up the error to an honest mistake?

"They also found the car used by the shooter's inside man. Someone torched it. They're sorting through what's left. Lost cause, though."

She thought of the shooter's driver parked at the loading dock and that strange blond hair, certain now it was a wig.

Amber wondered what would have happened if she had gone over Ibsen's head to the head of the business office upstairs, and sadness threatened to swallow her up.

Carter slid orange juice before her. "Drink that," he ordered. Then he returned his attention to Kurt. "Did they find the US marshals?" asked Carter, his face grim.

"Thanks to your marker."

"Anything on the two that impersonated the FBI?" asked Carter. "The ones who took Amber and me from the station?"

Kurt shook his head.

"Might be the same guys," offered Carter.

"That's what Jack thinks, too," said Kurt.

"How long have you been looking for us, Kurt?" asked Amber.

"I got a call from Jack yesterday about one in the afternoon saying that you two never made it to Phoenix. State Police, sheriff and police out of Darabee PD were all searching for you, but they didn't see the marker. You left that for us, right?"

Carter nodded and measured out the water, then poured it into the reservoir, then flipped on the coffeemaker. The hissing and gurgling sounded promising.

"Jack spotted that and called Tommy." Kurt flicked his attention to her. "He's a tracker with the Shadow Wolves."

Carter had told her that.

Kurt continued. "He's home on leave until the end of the month." His attention returned to Carter. "Anyway, by the time Tom got down there, the state police and FBI had ruined any tracks around the van. US Marshals had also been tromping around. Crime tape, the whole deal. They let Jack in since he found the thing, and that FBI guy, Forrest, he okayed us. He's Black Mountain, you know?"

"Met him," said Carter.

"They had seen where you went down the bank and brought the dogs who, of course, caught both trails and wanted to go in both directions at once. Tommy found your message, and we headed back toward town while the rest of them went the other way. But we lost you on the outskirts when you left the arroyo."

The coffeepot was only half full, but Carter tugged it free and half filled three mugs. He gave her one first.

"Sugar," he said, pointing to the packets in a similar mug on the table.

"Now you," said Kurt to Carter.

Carter rolled his shoulder and winced. "We were attacked by two gunmen driving an SUV with state police markings. Amber saw only one man. It was the same man from the copper mine," he said as he related the details of their experience.

After some questions, Carter continued and told how they'd returned to get the second pistol from the dead US marshal.

"Tommy said you had been back," Kurt said as his smile fell. "Is that when you got shot?"

"No. During a second attack. We stole a car. Left it behind in—"

"Found it already," said Kurt. "How'd you get here?"

Carter told him about the truck and asked if Kurt could get Jack to contact the owner and return the vehicle.

"I'm sure he can. Hey, that rental you were in was pretty banged up. Looked like you got hit from behind and sideswiped by a dark blue car."

"It hit us. Then he tried to knock us off the road, but I managed to push him off the shoulder. That's when I got shot."

"You see the driver?" he asked.

Carter shook his head and then lifted his chin toward Amber. "She did."

Kurt had set aside his coffee, and his expression was uneasy. "Same guy?"

Amber shook her head. "No. Not the shooter."

"Could you identify him?"

"Yes. He drove the Subaru the day we were kidnapped. Last night I saw him again, only his nose is all swollen, purplish." She thought of the man who had been driving the Subaru, picturing him as he stepped from the SUV and then with his nose gushing blood from the impact with the air bag. Her skin prickled. Something had been familiar about him. Was he the same one driving the van in Lilac? She briefly considered that and decided they could be one and the same.

Kurt turned back to Carter who had finished his coffee and was reaching for more.

"What kind of vehicle hit you?"

"A police cruiser, dark color. Bumped us from behind and then swiped Amber's door."

Kurt sagged back against the counter.

"What's wrong?" asked Carter.

"I saw that car."

"Where?"

"On the reservation last night. Unmarked car with the mirror hanging off. It was all scraped up on the driver's side."

"Tell Jack," said Carter.

"Yeah. I did." Kurt's hand ran absently through his thick short hair. "I forgot to tell you that the van they found at Lilac was outfitted with a police scanner."

Carter shifted from side to side as if trying to find his balance. "So they have been following all radio communication."

"That's what Jack said. He's got ears." Kurt lifted his coffee and drank the remains in one swallow. "This is why they can't find him."

Amber knew who he meant. It was impossible for the Lilac Mine shooter to still be at large and switching vehicles as if he owned a car rental company, unless he had help—the kind of help that came from law enforcement.

Chapter Twenty-Two

Carter's brother showered and changed. He didn't say anything about the bed that had obviously been slept in by two people, and when he was done, he gave Carter a container holding the rest of the antibiotic capsules.

"I'd like to bring you to the fire station," Kurt said. "Safer than here, I think."

But he wasn't sure. Amber could see that from his wrinkled brow.

He continued. "I don't want to leave you here alone." His hand went to his phone and then dropped away as he recalled it was no longer a viable option.

Carter shook his head. "Whoever is after us has information from the inside."

"Jack couldn't get that kind of detail," said Kurt.

Someone higher up than a tribal detective, thought Amber.

"What do you want me to do?" asked Kurt, reverting to little brother.

"Get to Ray, Dylan or Jack. Make sure to relay what you told me about the vehicle you spotted on our Rez. Then tell them where we are and tell them to identify themselves before they come through that door."

Kurt nodded. "I'll be as quick as I can be." He let his

dog back inside and then gave him a quick pat. "Take care of my brother, Justice."

Carter stood facing the closed door with the dog standing before him, tail wagging merrily. At least one of them was happy to be here.

Amber fiddled with her empty coffee mug as silence descended on the kitchen. She felt the gnawing ache that followed a mistake of epic proportions. Carter needed this reservation like he needed air. She knew she couldn't take him from this place. To experience how hard it was on the outside. How could she protect him the way he was protecting her?

Last night had proved two things. She still loved Carter, and she would have to leave him again to keep him safe.

She rose and took her mug to the sink. Carter intercepted her before she could get past him. His fingers wrapped about her forearm, staying her. She kept her eyes down.

"Amber? You okay?"

She thought of all the times she wasn't okay, back when her dad had disowned her, when she had to leave with nothing, when she'd come back to Carter and he'd rejected her, too. But of all those miserable times, this was the worst. Because she knew now that Carter understood everything and that they might have had a chance together in any other time and place. She gave one hard swallow, and she lifted her chin to face him.

"Fine."

He assessed her, studying her expression and staring into her eyes. She managed a half smile.

"Help is on the way," she said. And with it, their imminent separation.

He nodded, but kept hold of her with his hand and the steady stare.

"You want to talk about last night?"

A pain stabbed across her stomach, and she forced herself to relax, breathe, think.

She shook her head, not trusting her voice. Her jaw clamped so tight it ached.

His eyes narrowed. "Amber?"

She tried for a smile and from his growing concern, failed miserably.

"Say something," he demanded.

"I—I think you… I need a shower."

She had changed direction mid-sentence, but he didn't press.

"All right."

He let her ease past him and watched as she disappeared into the bathroom.

Despite his denial, he recognized what this was. Nine years had taught him that he wasn't going to ever get over her. Amber was too smart, too beautiful and too brave for him to chalk her up as something ordinary. She was exceptional in every way. She had fortitude and kept her wits under fire. She'd been strong enough to survive two dysfunctional parents and protect her sisters from their immorality. And he knew that she still had feelings for him even before last night. But he also knew she was holding back, and it scared him to death that she might be preparing to leave him again. She had tried to explain that she had left to protect him from making a mistake, taking on her father's debt and so becoming a partner in the crime of hurting her sisters. She had left them all out of love. The trouble she faced now was far worse. But if she still loved him, would that make her stay or go?

Carter pressed both hands to the kitchen counter and groaned. His head sank as he accepted the truth. He still loved Amber Kitcheyan.

She was the one for him. Now he had to figure out a way to keep her alive long enough to convince her to stay.

Carter headed into his brother's room. What would Amber wear? Some searching turned up a T-shirt from high school that must have been kept for nostalgic reasons. Carter packed his bag with food and water, then put both pistols in the bag.

The shower had stopped, so he knocked. "I set out some things on Kurt's bed."

She called her thanks, and he retreated to the kitchen to make breakfast. The first omelet burned a little, so he ate that one and then made another.

She emerged shortly afterward with her hair in two neat braids, flushed cheeks and smelling like his brother's deodorant. Unfortunately, that didn't dampen his reaction to the sight of her, clean and her skin pink and dewy.

She held out her arms, showing rolled cuffs at wrist and ankle, her scuffed high boots now under the denim cuffs. The jeans needed cinching at the middle but stretched across her backside in a way that made his eyebrows lift and his throat go dry.

"That will do," he said.

"Hungry?" he asked. At her nod he used the spatula to give her the second cheese omelet with more coffee. Then he hit the shower, which he found as challenging as getting dressed, thanks to his injury.

When he returned to her she gave him an odd look.
"You okay?" she asked. "You look a little green."

"I'm fine."

"They should be here soon," she said. "You don't have a fever, do you?" She carried her plate to the sink and then used the back of her hand to feel his forehead. "You'll probably need a tetanus shot or something."

"Kurt mentioned that."

Her cool hand brushed his forehead, and she frowned. Then she lifted up on tiptoes, grabbed him behind the neck and tugged. He folded obediently at the waist, and she pressed her lips to his forehead, then dropped back to her heels.

"You feel a little hot," she said.

"Every time I get close to you," he muttered.

Her gaze flashed to his, and perhaps she could see that he was not flirting because she only stared up at him with wide almond-shaped eyes.

"Me, too" she whispered.

Bad time to take her back to bed and a really, really bad time to share his feelings for her. But what if he didn't have another chance? They might not be alone again for who knows how long.

"Amber," he said, trying not to think too hard. He was better on the fly. "About last night."

She continued to stare, her dark eyes unreadable, but the tension in her mouth was not encouraging.

"Yes?"

"Well, I'm not leaving you, and I won't let them take you from me."

"They will take me, and if there is witness protection, then they'll separate us. They told me that."

"Not if you marry me."

She gaped. It took her a full half minute to close her mouth. Was it really that preposterous?

"No," she said at last.

"Why, no?"

"Because you're not leaving the reservation."

"I am if you are."

She turned away and then rounded on him. "Carter, every time you get near me, someone tries to kill us."

"And you think that's my fault?"

"Of course not. But you took a bullet yesterday. I can't live with that."

"You know what I can't live with?"

She waited, saying nothing.

"Losing you again. I am not losing someone else I love, and I am not leaving you behind like Hatch. That is not going to happen. Like it or not, you are stuck with me."

From beneath the table Justice growled and rose to his feet. Amber stiffened as the dog began to bark. Someone was here.

Chapter Twenty-Three

Carter reached behind his back, drawing out the pistol. He lifted his index finger to his lips and motioned Amber to move out of the kitchen, which she did as fast as her wobbly legs would carry her.

The breakfast that had tasted so good had started roiling in her stomach like a tumbleweed in high winds.

She hunched behind the wall, peeking back at Carter as he crept over to the door, and in a fast motion he glanced out before ducking behind the frame. Justice's growl grew louder, but Carter shushed him and Justice ceased his noise.

"Tribal PD," he said to her in a strained whisper.

His brother, probably. Or someone in another stolen car? she wondered, crouching lower behind the wall and knowing from the nightly news that Sheetrock made a terrible barrier against bullets.

Amber waited as the sound of doors shutting reached her. Then the murmur of voices.

A male voice called a greeting in Tonto Apache from outside. Amber knew that deep voice. It was Detective Jack Bear Den. She watched Carter's face for confirmation.

His shoulders sagged, and he lowered his weapon. He met her gaze and nodded, his mouth quirking upward.

From outside came more voices. Someone else spoke. They asked permission to enter. They told them to step away from the door. Carter issued a formal invitation to enter as he moved to the hall beside her, offering a hand as she rose to stand with him.

A moment later four men entered with weapons drawn but lowered. First came Jack Bear Den, filling the frame with his massive shoulders. He was followed by Ray Strong and Dylan Tehauno. Tribal Thunder had arrived. Finally Kurt Bear Den appeared at the rear and a surprise guest, Field Agent Luke Forrest.

Carter gave Jack a look.

"He's okay," said Jack, but Carter seemed unconvinced.

Jack holstered his pistol and came forward, resting a hand on Carter's injured shoulder. "You all right?"

"Yeah. What's going on?"

"We're bringing you to our station for now." Jack glanced at Amber and then returned his attention to Carter. "Kurt told me about the unmarked car, and he said that you've been shot."

Carter tugged at the collar of his shirt to show the bandage.

"He also said that Ms. Kitcheyan saw the man who shot you."

"I did."

"That makes you a VIP witness, Ms. Kitcheyan," said Luke Forrest. "You've seen the copper mine shooter, his driver and now a third man. You are sure he wasn't one of the other two?"

"I've been thinking about that. He might be the same man who drove the van in Lilac, and he was definitely the man driving the Subaru that took us from the tribal police station."

"The one with the busted nose?" asked Forrest.

Amber nodded. "No cap. No blond hair."

"We'll need your help for a new set of composite drawings. I have a call in to send one of our artists."

"You two ready?" asked Dylan.

Carter hoisted his bag and followed them out.

At the station, Kurt changed Carter's soggy dressing and checked the twelve stitches in his throbbing shoulder.

They were both questioned separately again. Each had some time with a technician trained to use the software program to create computer-based facial composites of both the copper mine shooter and his driver and the man who shot at them last night.

Jack had been with the FBI and Amber, but he returned to Carter with some news.

"Amber's composite of the shooter looks a lot like the man Kurt described seeing in the battered police unit, right down to the busted nose."

"Same guy?"

"Yeah. They think so. We're searching for the cruiser."

Carter mentioned the truck he had stolen again and Jack assured him it was on its way back to its owner with appologies and thanks.

"I'm taking lunch orders," said Jack. "What do you want?"

It was past three and closer to dinner than lunch.

"Jack, how long am I going to be sitting in this office?"

"We're making arrangements, Carter. But we want to be careful."

Carter raked his hands through his hair, ignoring the complaint from his healing shoulder.

"Maybe I am going crazy. But I think I'm…"

"Don't say it," said Jack, hand raised to stop him. "She's a witness."

"We're both witnesses."

"Do you get what's happening? They're not going to put you two up in some ski chalet in Vail. You two are leaving this Rez, and I might not even be able to find you."

Carter's hands dropped to his sides. "What are you talking about?"

"Protection. The kind that you don't get to opt out of."

"But we'll be together."

Jack rolled his eyes. "They'll separate you two for sure."

Carter sat back, his worst fears confirmed. "I can't let them take her again."

"Again? She left on her own the last time."

"It's complicated."

Jack sat back. "Yeah."

Carter thumped back in his seat. "I gotta think."

"I'm getting you a burger and fries. You want anything else?"

Besides Amber? "No."

Kurt delivered the meal and sat with Carter as he ate.

"Sorry about breaking into your place," said Carter to Kurt.

"I'm glad you did. Glad, you know, that you're all right."

His brother had been through a long night of worry. Carter felt badly about that, too.

"I couldn't think of a way to let you know."

"I understand. You did the right thing. Scared me, though."

"Yeah. I'm sorry."

Kurt didn't reply. Instead he pressed his lips tight and nodded, his eyes glassy. He breathed in and out and then nodded a few times, gathering himself.

"Amber gave me the papers to apply for reinstatement in the tribe."

Carter perked up. "That's good."

"Yeah," he said.

Just then the door flew open, and Dylan stood in the gap.

"They got him," he said. "The copper mine killer is in police custody."

THEY CAUGHT THE Lilac Mine Killer, as the press had dubbed him. Amber heard that he was on his way to the larger jail in Darabee. She and Carter would be making an ID there just as soon as they could arrange a lineup and safe transport.

The responsibility of that weighed on her. She knew the killer's face. She was very good with faces, though the names sometimes escaped her. And this face, the one gripping that huge rifle and looking right at her, was one she knew she would never forget.

Carter's brother returned with four officers. "You two ready?"

Amber stood stiffly, feeling awkward in the body

armor they had insisted she wear. The twinge of both her shoulder and hip ached from yesterday's collision. They told her that the bruised muscles had tightened up. They complained with each stride but loosened by slow degrees until she was seated again, in the back of a tribal police cruiser.

"They got him?" asked Carter.

"Seems so," Jack said.

"Will I be behind glass when I see him?" asked Amber.

"Yes," said Detective Bear Den. "They have a one-way mirror in their station. Buckle up, Ms. Kitcheyan."

Amber repressed a groan as she twisted to retrieve the shoulder restraint and clip it into place.

The drive to Darabee, some thirty minutes east, was uneventful. She tried and failed to spot the place where Carter had left the marker and had almost given up when she saw the yellow police tape fluttering from orange traffic cones by the side of the road. She said a prayer for the two US marshals killed while trying to protect them.

When they reached the station, it was twilight, but there was a great deal of light coming from the parking area beside the station. She couldn't make out what it was at first, but then she recognized the news vans with raised satellite antennae. It was clear from the bright floodlights and the press waiting with cameras poised that someone had leaked the arrest information to the news.

"Oh, great," said Jack.

"Sit tight," said Dylan, from the front passenger seat. "They have a back entrance. Darabee police are waiting to escort us in."

He passed a blanket back to each of them. They were the kind of fleece blankets you wrap around yourself at a football game, but they were blue and said FBI on them.

"These go over your heads. We don't want any photos of either of you."

She looked at Carter for rescue, and he said nothing as he unfolded the blanket. It was in that instant that Amber realized that her life would never go back to normal. Not ever.

AMBER MANAGED TO make it inside without tripping. Two athletic lawmen had held her by each arm, and she thought that her feet had barely touched the ground between the car and the neighboring police station in Darabee. She had been aware of the bright lights of the television cameras as she was rushed inside the station.

Once inside she was escorted to an interview room. There she clutched an unwanted foam cup of strong coffee as she waited to be called to identify their suspect. Both she and Carter would be called separately to make the identification from a lineup. They were told to take their time and be certain of their choice. The longer she sat here, the more nervous she became.

There would be only one opportunity to get it right. Carter would go first.

When they came for him, she stood, realizing that she would be left alone in this tiny interrogation room in his absence, and felt a rising sense of panic.

Carter gave her a warm, reassuring smile. "Be right back."

She fidgeted in the small room, drumming her fingers on the surface of the table that was bolted to the floor. She kept her eyes pinned on the door. Amber knew she should wait, but she found herself opening the door. Posted outside was a uniformed police officer, his matching blue shirt and slacks separated by a utility belt fixed with various tools of the trade. He looked surprised at her emergence. Beyond him she saw a man with a purple bruise on his face duck out of sight. Her mind flashed to an image of Carter kicking their captor in the face with his boot and their captor slapping a hand over his left eye. She lifted a finger to ask who that was.

"Ma'am?" he said. "I have to ask you to wait inside."

Could that have been the one that identified himself as Agent Muir? She knew it unlikely that the FBI impersonator was hanging out in the Darabee police station, but still, he was about the right height...and that shiner.

She turned her attention to the officer guarding the door and was about to tell him what she saw when there was a sharp report from a pistol.

The officer pushed her across the threshold as she heard the sound of more shots fired in close succession. One, two. Amber's flesh went cold. The officer's eyes rounded, and he drew his gun, gripping it with both hands. Then he hesitated.

"Stay there." He shut the door in her face. She heard a click and watched him run down the hall and out of sight.

Amber tried the door and found it locked.

She was trapped.

CARTER WAS IN the squad room. It was his understanding that the other men who would join the lineup were ready, and he was waiting only for the suspect to arrive. He was chatting with his brother when the shots sounded. His very first thought was of Amber.

Where was she?

Both he and Jack stood and Jack drew his weapon before they charged out into the hall. Carter found a scene of chaos before him. Officers shouted and tussled. He saw raised arms and the barrel of a gun pointed at the ceiling. Another shot discharged from the weapon. A young officer rushed past him. The same one that he had seen guarding Amber.

Jack looked at him, and Carter cursed. Jack went toward the shots, and Carter headed in the opposite direction at a run.

Carter reached the interrogation room to find no guard posted. Amber pounded on the locked door and shouted to let her out. He tried the knob, releasing the button that locked the door. Amber spilled out and into his arms.

"What's happening?" she cried.

"Don't know." He wrapped an arm about her and hurried her farther into the station, heading for the small kitchenette they had passed on arrival.

She clung to him as they ran through the open door which he closed behind them. The windowless staff room contained a microwave, sink, refrigerator and three small circular tables with plastic chairs. The walls were decorated with safety awareness posters. Amber didn't step away from him but continued to grip the fabric of his shirt in her fists.

"Get behind me," he ordered.

She hesitated only a moment and then did as he asked.

"Do you still have a weapon?" she asked.

"They took it." He motioned to the counter and sink that jutted from the wall. "Back behind that."

Amber wedged herself into the gap between the white refrigerator and end of the countertop with the wood grain Formica finish. Carter flicked off the lights and watched the door.

"What should we do?" she whispered.

"Wait."

They listened in silence to the voices. There were no more shots. Carter glanced to Amber who now squatted with one hand on the refrigerator and the other gripping the edge of the counter.

She told him about the man she glimpsed, the one with the black eye.

"You think it was Muir?"

She nodded.

This didn't make any sense. They were in a police station. They were supposed to be safe.

Someone opened a door down the hall. Carter couldn't see who without revealing their position.

"She's not here," said the unfamiliar voice. Was it the officer assigned to protect her or someone else?

Carter lifted a finger to his lips, and Amber nodded.

He backed away from the door as the footsteps approached. Doors opened. The footsteps again. A heavy tread. The door burst open, and Carter sprang. The intruder flicked on the light before Carter hit him in the chest carrying them both into the hall.

AMBER CROUCHED AGAINST the wall. She could see Carter's legs but not the man in the hall.

"I'm a cop," said the downed man.

"What are you doing?" asked Carter.

Amber moved out to see Carter gripping the lapels of the man's blazer in both fists.

"Looking for the woman. The idiot plebe left her."

Amber recognized a Texas accent, and her skin prickled. She stood and peered around the refrigerator to see an Anglo man in a dress shirt, slacks and tie, now askew. A badge was clipped to his hip beside his empty holster. The man's gaze flicked to her. Carter's gaze did not waver, so he must have seen the odd look the man cast her. She couldn't define it, but thought it seemed a sort of triumph, like a boy finding the last person in a game of hide-and-seek.

His attention shifted to Carter. "I said I'm a police officer. Detective Casey, DPD."

"Get my brother," ordered Carter.

"I have to take y'all somewhere secure," he said.

Carter didn't move. Had he picked up the accent?

"We're secure. Now get my brother."

"Y'all need to give me my gun back."

Carter shook his head and aimed the gun at the detective.

"It's a crime, what you're doing."

Carter didn't move, and he didn't lower his gun.

Detective Casey pursed his lips and blasted a great exhalation of breath.

"My brother?" Carter prompted.

"Sure."

He retreated a step. Amber wanted to ask what was happening but also did not want that man to linger any longer.

Finally Casey released the door and stepped out of sight. Carter did not holster his weapon. Instead he took a position before her, pressing her body against the wall.

"Texas accent," she said.

"Yeah," he replied.

The voices outside had quieted, and so it was easy to hear the footsteps. More than one person, she judged. Amber drew a breath and held it. Who was out there now?

"Carter? Amber? It's Jack. Are you two still in there?"

Amber's shoulders sagged, and the wind left her. She wrapped her arms about Carter's middle and pressed her cheek to his broad muscular back.

"Yes," he called, making his voice vibrate against her face.

"Can we come in?"

"Who?"

"Me, Forrest, Chief Tinnin and Detective Casey from Darabee."

"Just you," replied Carter.

Amber released him, coming to stand at his side. Carter lowered his weapon.

Jack entered, and Carter holstered his gun. Jack made a face.

"I have to take that," he said, motioning to the pistol holstered at Carter's hip.

"I don't think so," said Carter.

"You almost shot one of their officers."

Carter shook his head. "Guy had a Texas accent."

Jack's brow quirked, and Amber knew he understood the implications of that.

"What happened out there?" asked Carter.

Jack rubbed his neck as he answered. "Someone shot our suspect."

"Shot?" said Carter. "In a police station. How would that happen?"

"Happened to Lee Harvey Oswald."

Carter glared.

Jack filled them in. "Just outside the station, as they were bringing him in," said Jack.

"They brought him in the front door?" asked Carter.

"We didn't. It was Darabee's bust, and they wanted to show him off."

"So they brought him past the news cameras."

Jack looked positively grim during his explanation.

"We have his killer in custody," said Jack.

"Well, hurrah," said Carter.

"What about the suspect?" asked Amber.

"Dead."

"Jack, Amber thinks she saw the guy that took us. The one I kicked in the eye."

"Where?"

Chapter Twenty-Four

Carter paced from one side of the small staff room to the other. The FBI and Darabee PD had searched the station for the man Amber said she saw but came up empty. If he had been here, he was here no longer.

Agent Forrest had joined them as well as Tribal Chief Tinnin and the Darabee chief of police, Jefferson Rowe. Amber sat at one of the lunch tables, and he stood next her. Jack flanked Amber's other side as they faced Forrest, Rowe and Tinnin.

"That's just great," said Carter. "The shooting suspect is dead, and you can't find the two men who kidnapped us yesterday."

"What about the guy, the one who came to the door? He had a Texas accent."

"Yeah," said Chief Rowe. "He's one of mine. Detective Eli Casey. He came to find you two when your guard left his post."

Carter and Jack exchanged a look. Having a Texas accent wasn't a crime, but he knew Jack was on it.

"He have a brother?" asked Jack.

Rowe's eyes narrowed. "Not sure. Why?"

Amber broke in. "But he's dead. The shooter from

Lilac, I mean. So they don't need us as witnesses. Right? We can go home."

Carter glanced at Amber and saw the weariness in her posture and in the dark smudges under her eyes.

"We still need you," said Forrest. "We need a positive ID on the suspect to start."

"But he's…" Amber's eyes widened and then her gaze flashed to Carter. He made it to her in two steps and grabbed a hold of her arm as she swayed. She slipped her hands around his biceps and squeezed. He tried to ignore the aching want that she triggered. Amber was done in by a day that would bring most women to hysterics.

"We can use photos," said Forrest, talking fast, his hands raised to assuage Amber's obvious agitation.

"You don't have to view the body," added Rowe.

At the word body, Amber's strength finally went out. Carter caught her, drew her in and held on.

"We'd like to move you back to the…ah, the room you just vacated," said Forrest.

"The interrogation room? The one that locks from the outside?" asked Carter. "Nope. That won't work for us. Bring the photos here. And get Amber a water or something."

Carter helped Amber to a seat at one of the circular tables and drew up a chair next to her. She sagged against him, and he curled an arm around her waist.

"I've never seen a dead body," she whispered.

"I'll be right here."

He glanced at Rowe who shook his head. "She needs to make the ID separately from you."

Amber shuddered and buried her face in Carter's chest. He stroked her head as she struggled to bring her breathing back under control. The water arrived in a plastic bottle, and Carter coaxed her to drink. By slow degrees she pulled herself together. She sipped her water, and Carter kept an arm around her narrow shoulders and his eyes on her.

"It will be all right," he said.

She turned her dark, worried eyes on him. "Will it?"

He nodded. "I'm not letting you go, Amber. We'll get through this together."

By the time Jack returned with Tinnin, Amber was sitting erect with an expression of grim determination on her face. He'd seen that same expression on his mother's face before she went in for some outpatient surgery. It was that "let's get this over with" look.

Jack spoke in a soothing tone, or what passed for soothing. Jack's voice was too gruff to be comforting, but he managed to kick it down from threatening to neutral.

"They have the photos ready," said Jack. "Carter, you're first."

Carter stood. "I'm not leaving her alone."

"I'll…" Jack turned to the door. "I'll stay. Two of Rowe's men have the door. That work?"

"That guy Casey doesn't come in here," said Carter.

"All right," said Rowe.

"Then I'll be quick." He turned to Amber. "You be all right?"

She lifted her chin and gave a stiff little nod. He'd never met a braver woman. Damn but she was magnificent.

With that he gave Amber's hand a squeeze and followed Chief Rowe out to see if he could make an ID of the prime suspect in the Lilac Copper Mine shooting.

AMBER WAS ABSOLUTELY certain that she'd have nightmares featuring those faces for a long time to come.

Amber had been nervous about the ID. But it was simple to spot the man who she had seen outside Mr. Ibsen's home and again yesterday afternoon. The harder part was knowing that she looked at the face of a dead man. They were all dead, each photo of a man about the same age, weight and ethnicity and all a little too pale, grayish and glassy-eyed to still be breathing.

"That's just great," said Jefferson Rowe, the chief of the Darabee police force. He seemed to realize he needed a shave, because he scratched at the whiskers that were mostly black.

"Is that all?" she asked.

He gave her a long look. "All for now. I'm sure the Feds will be taking you to a safe house. We've suggested a few spots, but I think they're going back to the same hotel you were in on Tuesday night. Nice place, I hear."

She didn't like his smile, and it took a moment to realize that was because it didn't reach his eyes. They were a glacial blue and just as welcoming.

The chief glanced at Field Agent Forrest, but he neither confirmed nor denied Rowe's surmise. Now Amber did smile at Forrest's poker face.

"Can I ask you about the man who killed him?" asked Amber.

The chief's jaw pulsed as his teeth came together.

"Active investigation," he said.

Of course the shooting had happened on this man's watch, right here in front of his police station. Judging by the color of his face, he found that embarrassing, and well he should.

Forrest led her out, and a second federal officer flanked her other side as they walked down the hall.

"His name is Karl Hooke," said Forrest, answering her question. "And he's a member of the Turquoise Canyon Tribe."

"What?" She couldn't believe that. It made no sense for someone from their tribe to want to murder the man who attacked a copper mine. "Did he have family there, in Lilac?"

Forrest shook his head.

"Then why?"

Agent Forrest took her elbow and guided her along. "We aim to find out."

She stopped. "Wait. Hooke. Not Morgan Hooke's father."

Forrest narrowed his eyes on her. "He has one child. A daughter, and her name is Morgan."

Amber reeled. "I know her. Or I did know her, in high school."

Agent Forrest did not seem to like that at all.

"You know her father."

"No, not really. Just by sight."

"So he wasn't the driver or one of the men who abducted you?"

She shook her head. "Those men were Anglos."

When she returned to the kitchenette, it was to find Carter and Jack Bear Den conversing in Apache. Carter was in body armor again, which meant they were moving.

Carter broke away to greet her, taking both her icy hands in his. Just the sight of him made everything seem better.

"How did it go?"

"Good," said Forrest for her. "She ID'd the same photo. We're confirming with latents we have recovered, but we are reasonably sure he's the one."

"What about the other men?" she asked. "His driver and the man who hit us last night."

Forrest stopped talking so Jack answered. From Agent Forrest's sour look she assumed he did not approve.

"We have a suspect. Searching for him now," said Jack.

And if they found him, they could find the other man.

"That's good," she said finally allowing herself to smile. "Very good."

Jack seemed to want to say more, but Forrest stepped between them.

"For tonight we are bringing you to a safe house. It's more secure than a hotel."

"Where?" she asked.

"It's on Turquoise Canyon Rez. We need you to put on this vest."

She'd worn the same vest on the trip here from Turquoise Canyon. She accepted Carter's help suiting up in the body armor. They waited while final arrangements were made. Then they were led through the prisoner holding area and out through a side entrance to a waiting van. There Chief Rowe and several officers guarded the exit. By the vehicle waited two more unfamiliar FBI agents in blue windbreakers with bold yellow lettering announcing their affiliation. Amber gave them a good looking over, but there seemed nothing obvious out of order. Still she wouldn't relax until she was back in some kind of building, preferably one on tribal land and with a steel door.

Carter and Jack both stopped at once.

She followed the direction of their gaze. They both gaped at the vehicle. This time they were moving in a Hummer. The really big kind.

Amber glanced from one to the other. Both men had gone pale, and she recalled Carter telling her of the night they lost Hatch. They'd been in Humvees. Was that the same thing?

"Carter?" she said, taking his elbow.

He glanced at her, his face now covered with sweat.

"You okay?" she asked.

"Get in, Mr. Bear Den," said Agent Forrest, his gaze shifting from them to scan the area. Amber understood the message. They were in danger here.

"Carter, we have to go," she said.

He nodded and took a hesitant step forward.

Jack did not move. She glanced back. "I'll follow," he said.

He wasn't getting in that Hummer. She could tell by the rounding of his eyes and his stiff frame. It was the first time she'd ever seen them afraid. Both of them.

She helped Carter up and followed. Was she sitting in the spot where Hatch Yeager had been or was Carter?

"Let's go," she said, still holding Carter's arm.

Forrest stood next to the opened side door. "What's wrong?"

"Insurgents attacked Carter and his brother in this sort of vehicle."

Forrest swore.

Once they were both inside, the chief poked his head in, his smile broad and his blue eyes cold.

"Good luck, you two, and good job today." He turned to Agent Forrest, now moving up behind him. "Sure you shouldn't go to that hotel? Seems safer to stay put."

"No changes," said Forrest and swept up into the seat behind them.

"Well, we'll bring you to the boundary. Tinnin's guys will have to take it from there."

Carter's brother nodded, shouldering the responsibility, and then hurried off, wiping the sweat from his brow.

Forrest's partner climbed into the third row and closed the door. A few minutes later they were under way.

They had not left the police lot before Agent Forrest told them to move. He wanted them in the back and both on the floor.

"Why?" asked Carter.

"Theory we are working," said his partner.

"Too many people know where you were seated."

She thought of all the police officers from the station. Did they think someone there was involved?

Carter relocated first and sat on the floor, and she moved beside him. Forrest handed over helmets.

"Really?" said Carter. But when Forrest and his partner put one on, Carter fixed one on Amber's head and then his own.

"We have an escort?" asked Carter.

"Better," said Forrest.

The Hummer made a turn and Amber cuddled close to Carter who leaned against the door. He wrapped her up in his arms and pulled her onto his lap. Somehow the beating of his heart was more comforting than the Kevlar and helmet.

"You okay?" she whispered.

He pressed his nose into her neck and inhaled. "Now I am."

"Going to be a long ride this way," she said to their escorts.

"If we're right it won't be long," said Forrest.

"You want to fill us in down here?" said Carter.

"Your brother, Jack, remembered Orson Casey because he arrested him once on tribal land. D and D. Texas boy, Bear Den said. Jack says he had priors. After the arrest, Orson's brother came for him. Name's Eli and he's a police officer in Darabee."

Amber didn't like the sound of that.

"What were the priors?" asked Carter.

"Different things. Escalating. Worst was manslaughter," said Forrest.

"So why is he walking around loose?" asked Carter.

"Witness, uh, failed to make an ID."

"You mean somebody got to the witness."

"Probably. Eli, we think."

"Who did Orson kill?" asked Carter.

"Car dealership night cleaning person. Orson Casey is alleged to have burned down the dealership."

"Why?" asked Carter.

"Member of WOLF, and they object to gas guzzling cars."

"Like this one?" asked Amber.

"Quiet now, we're almost there."

"Almost where?"

"Boundary to your reservation."

They continued to speed along the road. Amber looked up and out the window.

"Going dark," said the agent driving. The headlights flicked off with the dash lights.

"What's happening?" she asked.

Carter held her tighter.

The stars were clear through the large window, pinpoints of blue through the tinted glass. Then something large came up beside them. They swerved to make room and then bumped along the opposite shoulder, slowing, turning, leaving the road.

They came to a stop.

"We left the convoy?" she asked.

"Yes."

"Why?"

"Sending a decoy in our place," said Forrest.

"That's dangerous," said Amber.

Carter chuckled. "You weren't worried when it was us in there."

"No. I was worried."

"Sit tight," said Forrest. "We've got an army out here with us. You can't see them, but they're here. And if anything is going to happen to the convoy, it will be soon."

Amber nestled against Carter who toyed with her hair. When his fingers brushed her neck, she let the tingle of pleasure slip over her skin. Electricity, she thought, every time he touched her.

The radio in the dash crackled. "Shots fired."

Silence again.

"In pursuit."

Amber felt the helicopter that passed overhead. But

she didn't see it. The vibrations thudded through her chest nearly as hard as her own heart.

"Suspect spotted," said another voice.

"In pursuit."

"One suspect in custody," came the newest update.

"How many are there?" said Forrest under his breath.

"Second suspect is down."

The driver cursed. "They better not have killed him."

It was a long silent stretch of dead air before they heard that they had apprehended Orson Casey. His brother, Officer Eli Casey, was dead.

Chapter Twenty-Five

Amber was so tired she was weaving on her feet by the time they arrived in the Phoenix federal building where an FBI field office was located. There she identified Orson Casey from a lineup. Carter made his selection afterward, and they were told they both fingered the same person.

So Orson Casey was the driver of the van in Lilac she saw on the loading dock and the driver of the Subaru impersonating an FBI officer. She also identified Orson as the man in the unmarked car who had shot Carter.

Amber had been shown a photo of Eli Casey, and her skin when icy at the sight. It was the detective at the station in Darabee, the one who had come searching for her during the shooting and who Carter had chased off.

"He was there to kill me, wasn't he?" she asked Carter.

"I think so," said Carter.

She had asked Agent Forrest about the man at the station with the black eye.

"Got him. We'll have you try to identify him pretty quick here."

"Who is he?"

"Name is Jessie Gillroy, and he is also with Darabee PD. A detective. Works with Eli Casey. Or he did. He's now in federal custody, and Eli is dead. Jessie's a match for the inside man at Lilac. Opened the doors for Sanchez. We think he and Orson Casey might help us discover who is funding this operation and where to find those missing explosives."

"Eli Casey and Jessie Gillroy both worked in Darabee?" Was that why Gillroy had looked familiar? Had he been there with Eli Casey and the others at the Darabee police department when she had arrived from Lilac with Carter via air ambulance? She clutched her arms about herself as a cold chill took hold.

Forrest nodded. "Rowe has some crooked officers up there. They've been taking payoffs from someone for information."

"Is that how they knew where to find us?"

Forrest nodded.

Amber wondered how Darabee detectives had gotten hold of a state police vehicle and known their whereabouts when they had been in the custody of US Marshals. She wanted to ask Carter about that because she didn't think a police officer could get ahold of that kind of information, which meant that someone else was involved. Someone higher up.

Plus, the man who had tried to coax her into that Subaru was still at large, and she was growing more certain he had been at the police station tonight.

She supposed that was for the FBI to unravel, and she was too fuzzy-headed to work anything else out. Still it bothered her. Something about it just felt wrong. Why go to so much trouble to kill her? The FBI was already investigating the supply chain at Lilac. What was the point of chasing after her? She didn't know anything.

Unless she did. She rubbed her tired eyes trying to think; she reviewed the sequence of events that had transpired as she'd done repeatedly since the shooting. She had told Ibsen about the overage in the delivery. He had seemed both distracted and upset. He'd told her he would take care of it and then shown her out. That was the last she'd seen him, wasn't it? Something nagged at her; she just couldn't think.

Agent Forrest sat with her in the cubicle where she'd been told to wait. This guy had about as much to say as his desk lamp, and he made her uncomfortable. But Carter trusted him. It was enough for her.

Forrest told her that the convoy with the decoy Hummer had been attacked by riflemen who took out both windows behind which she and Carter should have been seated. They'd used a caliber of bullet that went through protective glass. But they'd revealed their location, and the FBI had caught them. If they had not made the switch, Amber and Carter would both be lying beside Eli Casey in the morgue in Darabee.

"Why did they say their names were Muir and Leopold?" she asked. "Those are the names of famous environmentalists. Aren't they?"

"Very good. Muir founded the Sierra Club and Leopold founded the Wilderness Society."

She shook her head, bewildered. Why choose names of such men?

"So, did Orson tell you who Leopold really is?"

"Not yet." Forrest went quiet again, watching her.

"We believe evidence will show that the man claiming to be Muir was actually Gillroy."

"And the men who came after them. Two men, Jack told me. And I heard one say, 'get my brother.' So was that Eli Casey?"

"Yes. The other man is yet unidentified. Soon we hope."

"Who is Warren Cushing? That's what I read on the ID I found in his wallet when I was searching for the handcuff key."

"Cushing ran a tourist outfit in Sedona. Crimson Hummer Excursions. They take guests on off-road tours of the canyons and rock formations. He died two years ago. He'd just received permits for expansion and was murdered at his offices."

"How did he get Cushing's ID?"

"Trophy maybe. We are looking into that."

Then she remembered. A fire. Sedona. Off-road trips.

"I saw that on the news. It was arson. That fire, and the news said—" she reached back into her memory for the information "—some group claimed responsibility."

"WOLF," said Forrest, his whiskey eyes studying her.

Amber sat back. "The other FBI agents, the real ones who questioned me, they asked me about WOLF and BEAR."

"Yes, we thought you were affiliated."

She wasn't and had only attended the PAN rally because her uncle had invited her along.

Her uncle was the head of his medicine society, the one that Carter belonged to, and Carter had some special role there, Tribal Thunder, he said. That wasn't a part of these eco-extremists.

Amber rubbed her arms.

"Cold, Ms. Kitcheyan?"

She shook her head, her mouth now firmly sealed. What did her uncle have to do with all this?

She squeezed her eyes shut, praying that Carter was not tied up in this mess. That his interest in her was genuine and not because he was a part of some vigilante environmental army.

Amber was suddenly terrified that Forrest would mention her uncle's name as a suspect.

"Did they ever catch the arsonists?" asked Amber.

Forrest kept his gaze pinned on her as he shook his head.

She wanted to ask about her uncle, but she did not fully trust Forrest. He was Apache, but not of her tribe.

"Was it those people, the WOLF group, who attacked my office?"

"We believe it was BEAR. WOLF generally tries to avoid loss of life. BEAR makes no such allowances. They believe in the preservation of the environment at the expense of human life."

The mine shooting. She pressed both palms together and lifted them to her lips.

"They did it?"

Forrest nodded. "Yes, we do believe so. Ovidio Natal Sanchez is a known member of BEAR."

Was Carter involved? He'd been there and so fast. The coincidence seemed too unbelievable. Or was it her uncle who was involved or…or both?"

"Would you like some water?" he asked.

Amber turned to him. "We aren't waiting for Carter, are we?"

He shook his head. "No."

"This is an interrogation."

"Of sorts."

"Where's Carter?" she asked.

He didn't say anything. The door opened, and Agent Rose stepped in. His expression was like a guest in the receiving line at a funeral. Amber wrapped her arms around herself and rose to her feet.

"Where's Carter?"

"Amber, I think you should sit down," said Agent Rose. What was wrong with his lip? It looked split open.

She shook her head. Whatever he was going to tell her, it was bad. Really, bad.

"Is he all right?"

"Yes. Please, sit."

She shook her head, refusing his request a second time. "What's happening?"

"We've released him," said Agent Forrest.

"Released?" Her knees went wobbly.

Agent Rose got a hold of her and guided her to the chair he had tried to get her into.

"I—I don't understand," she said. Her ears were buzzing because she did understand. "We're in danger."

Forrest shook his head.

"He identified the shooter and that man is dead," said Forrest. "He identified the driver who abducted you, and that man is also dead."

"Leopold," she said.

"Not after him."

"But the extremist groups," she said.

"He seems to know nothing about that, and at present we have no reason to detain him. Chief Tinnin was insistent. He obtained a court order, and so we were compelled to release him."

Yet here she sat. Her skin went icy cold.

Her brain was trying to tell her something, but the fear and panic kept nosing it away, and she couldn't grab hold.

"But there might be more of them. They might hurt him."

"Very likely. But Mr. Bear Den appears to be no threat to anyone."

"He needs protection," she insisted. "Do you have men guarding him?"

"Watching him. Not guarding."

Rose dabbed at his oozing lip with a clean cloth.

"They shot him," she said, not liking the hysterical note in her voice.

"We believe you were the target," said Rose.

"And that you remain a threat to BEAR," said Forrest.

"How am I a threat?"

"That is why we are sitting here. You know something or saw something."

"I didn't."

Forrest shrugged. "We'll come round to it sooner or later."

Rose smiled, and his lower lip cracked open and began to bleed again.

Had Carter given him that fat lip?

Forrest spoke again. "For now you are a protected federal witness."

She shook her head in denial because she now realized that she was the target of all this. She was the last survivor from her office. The one who had spotted the discrepancy, seen the Lilac Mine shooter and at least three of the men who had been hunting her ever since. One remained at large. The pickup man with Eli Casey. Who was he? Where was he? And how many more were out there?

Amber stared from Rose to Forrest. She had never felt more alone in all her life. Rose offered her a paper cup of water, and she gulped down a few swallows before setting aside the cup that trembled in her hands.

"And now you need to come with us," said Rose.

She didn't want to but couldn't think of anything else to do. She didn't feel safe with them. She felt safe with Carter, and he was gone. Would she see him again?

"For how long?" she asked, rising to her feet. The men exchanged looks and tight expressions.

Witness protection. She knew it because they did not know who was in the extremist group called BEAR. They didn't know if the group would retaliate because of Eli Casey's death. They'd been willing to assassinate the Lilac shooter to prevent him from talking.

Amber had been cast out of her tribe many years ago. But she had still had her family. Now she was about to lose them and everything she was. She was about to become invisible.

Amber had lost control of her life once more, and yet now, as they led her away, she did not long for her mother or sisters. She longed for Carter Bear Den. She admitted to herself that she loved him still and that he was much safer without her.

CARTER GROWLED AT KURT. He'd already socked two FBI agents in the face, and Jack said he was lucky they didn't press charges. That only made him want to punch Jack, too, especially after his brother had bumrushed him into the waiting police unit, but no one punched Jack unless they needed the exercise.

Amber was back there in Phoenix, and when she returned from identifying the surviving Casey brother, she'd be upset, and he would not be there to comfort her. If Jack was right, the next and last time he would see Amber was at Orson Casey's trial.

"Almost home," said Jack.

Jack had navigated the switchbacks up the mountain and the long stretches beside the reservoirs until they had nearly reached the stretch of river and canyon that was theirs by federal treaty.

He was positive that the Casey boys had some serious help from someone, possibly more than one person in Darabee. Eli Casey had been a cop there, and Carter just knew there were more men involved. How else had they allowed a civilian into the station with a pistol and close enough to their shooting suspect to gun down Ovidio Natal Sanchez right there in front of the television cameras?

Sanchez's killer, their very own Karl Hutton Hooke, was an unemployed widower from Turquoise Ridge, the smallest of the Turquoise Canyon communities, and full-blood Apache. Carter felt sick over that. He wondered about the accomplice at the mine. The one who let the shooter in at the loading dock.

"Not Apache, thank the Lord," said Jack. "They found Ann-Marie Glenn's key card in Orson Casey's apartment. But he was the driver for Sanchez. Who let Sanchez in at the loading dock?"

Jack shrugged. "Eli or Jessie Gillroy, likely."

Carter sat back in his seat. That was for the FBI to untangle. Forrest had been very clear on that.

Jack had filled him in on a few missing details about the convoy attack and apprehension of the Casey boys.

Carter stared out Jack's cruiser as the light from the rising sun crept down the canyon wall, turning the rock face orange. Saturday morning, he realized, less than a week since he'd driven down to Lilac to deliver a message.

Was his truck still down there parked beside the helicopter pad?

He thought of Kenshaw Little Falcon and Forrest's implication that Amber's uncle might be involved in more than spiritual leadership of his tribe and their medicine society. Carter rubbed the tattoo on his right arm, bandaged now and the stitches were beginning to itch.

What was the purpose of Tribal Thunder? he wondered. To protect their land, of course. But how far was Little Falcon prepared to go to do that?

Forrest had told him last night that they didn't need him until the trial. Tribal leadership had involved their attorneys, who'd gained Carter's release because of the tribe's sovereign status; the FBI had agreed to release Carter if the tribe agreed not to get into a public pissing match over their star witness, Amber Kitcheyan. Who was fighting for her? Not her parents or her tribe. Nobody, that was who.

Carter had told them she had applied for reinstatement. Kurt had delivered the paperwork, but the tribal leadership had not yet readmitted her. And now they might never do so.

"But I'll see her at the trial."

Jack startled at the break in the long stretch of silence.

"I don't know."

His shoulder was throbbing, and the stitches tugged. He realized he'd forgotten to take his antibiotics. He fished in his pocket for the capsules Kurt had given him and downed one dry. It stuck in his throat.

"This is wrong."

"The FBI has this investigation. You're a tribe member so…"

Carter growled like an angry bear.

Jack blew out a breath. "Mom is worried sick. Dad said his hair is falling out because of all this. How about you let them see you in one piece? Then we can figure out what to do."

Carter folded his arms over his chest, winced in pain and lowered his elbow to the armrest.

"You don't understand. I might never see her again."

"She's safe, Carter, and she's not your responsibility anymore."

But he wanted her to be. He wanted to love her and protect her and be there.

"Listen, I know you like her, but she's a federal witness in a case that seems as though it is going to be huge. They finally have one of the eco-extremists. They hope that's just a start. You have to know that she's marked for witness protection. You can't go with her."

So why was he considering it?

Jack looked at him and then back to the road and then back to him again.

"Carter, you hear me? If you go with her, you will have to leave the tribe and your family. All of us. You won't be able to see us again, ever."

Carter swallowed at the magnitude of the decision he faced.

"Say something, brother."

He looked at Kurt. "I love her."

Jack swore.

CARTER'S MOTHER AND father met him at the door. All he saw of his mother was her arms outstretched as she threw herself at him. He hugged her and then hugged his father. His mother was not quite ready to let him go and maintained a firm grip on his hand as she drew him into his childhood home.

His mother's eyes were red, and his father's rugged face seemed older than he remembered. Thomas, Kurt and Jack entered the living room a moment later, and each received a similar hug from their parents. Jack had to stoop slightly to permit his mother to get her arms around his neck.

"So, our leadership worked it out," said his father to Jack.

"Yeah. We'll need to keep an eye on him. Chief Tinnin is worried about reprisals from the Casey family."

"But the copper mine shooter is dead, and the other two are arrested or dead," said his mother.

"There is at least one guy still out there," said Jack.

"I spoke to Kenshaw Little Falcon," said his father. "He feels that some are unhappy at recent events."

"Who?" asked Carter.

His father gave no answer.

"And the explosives are unaccounted for," said Jack.

"No question. Tinnin says the Feds are scrambling to find them and keep the disappearance secret."

His parents exchanged a long look.

"He's not safe here," said his mother in a whisper.

"We'll keep him safe," promised his father. It was a promise he might have a hard time keeping.

"It's happening again," whispered his mother.

Jack and Carter exchanged a confused look as their mother turned to her husband. "Was this a mistake? Taking him out of witness protection?"

Kurt spoke now. "If he enters witness protection, he's not coming back."

His mother rounded on him, her voice raised. "I know that! Don't you think I know that?" She sagged against her husband. "Not again," she whispered. "I can't lose Carter, too."

Jack's brow quirked. Carter shook his head at Jack's silent question. He had no idea what their mom was talking about. Had she said *again*?

When had this happened before? Carter was at a loss.

All four of her sons stepped back. Carter had never seen his mother act this way. Their father pulled her in close.

"It's all right, Mother," Carter said.

"No. It's not," she pressed her face into their dad's denim shirt, and it sounded like she said, "Not again."

Jack's and Carter's gazes met as if each wanted to know if the other had heard that.

"She'll be all right in a minute." Their dad wrapped an arm around his wife and patted her back. He spoke to her in Apache, calming words, tender words.

Carter was torn between the need to comfort and

reassure his mother and the need to tell them all what he had decided. He appreciated his tribe's intervention to get him released from federal protection, but he couldn't stay here. Not when Amber was there.

He cleared his throat, and all the males in the room looked to him.

"You should have asked me before you pulled me out."

"We've got your back," said Thomas. "I'm taking a leave to be with you."

He didn't want that. He didn't want his brothers to have to spend their lives guarding his.

"No. You're not. Because I'm not staying. I'm going back. It's the only way I know to keep you all safe and…"

His mother lifted her head and stared at him in absolute horror.

He faltered and then had to look away before he could continue. "I love Amber Kitcheyan. I'm not willing to let her go."

His dad stepped toward him, but his mother held him back.

"They'll separate you," said Jack.

"Not if I marry her."

Carter clamped his teeth together as he looked from one anxious face to the next. His family whom he loved stared at him in silence.

"You aren't safe with me here," he said, his voice taking on an unwelcome quaver. "And she needs me."

"You can't jump in and out of protective custody," said Jack. "We can't just return you like a dog to the pound."

"Then you better figure it out before the US Marshals take her again."

"I don't like it," said Jack.

"Neither do I. But it's my only choice."

His mother extended a hand, grasping his. "You could stay."

"Mom." He hugged her. "I can't."

She squeezed him so tight his neck ached and his shoulder throbbed.

Carter eased away, grateful to his dad for taking charge of his wife. Carter turned to Jack.

"Make a call, Jack. Tell them whatever you have to. Tell them there's been an attack, but get me back to her."

Chapter Twenty-Six

Two months later, Amber was preparing to testify. She should have been focusing on the upcoming trial and her small but vital part in the proceedings. Instead she was anticipating her meeting with Carter today.

After she had rested and had time to think over all that had happened she had recalled the phone conversation she had heard outside Ibsen's office the day before the shooting and given Forrest the name she had overheard—Theron Wrangler. Forrest had seemed stunned.

"Who is he?" she asked Field Agent Forrest.

"A documentary filmmaker, a political insider," he had said. "Since you mentioned him, we've identified several contacts between him and Harvey Ibsen."

"Is he involved in all this?"

Forrest's expression had given away nothing. "Ongoing investigation," was all he had said.

She took that to mean that Theron Wrangler was their new prime suspect.

She had asked Agent Forrest to allow her to see Carter Bear Den, and he had refused on every occasion. But with the trial approaching she had tried again and even refused to testify if she did not see Carter. Finally, Forrest agreed and arranged a meeting. Now here, she paced the inner chamber of the federal building like a caged lioness as she waited for Carter to appear.

She knew she would have only a few minutes and wondered how much she should say? The door opened, and she tried to hide her disappointment when Agent Forrest peered inside.

"Visitor for you," he said.

The next face she saw was the one she longed for. Carter stepped in, and the door closed behind him. She rushed three steps in his direction before regaining her composure. She walked the final few steps and clasped his hands.

"I'm so glad to see you."

"I saw your sisters and mom before I came. They are all well and send their love." He retrieved his hand, and she felt a tiny sting of sorrow.

Then he reached in his coat and passed her an envelope. "Photos of everyone and a letter from Kay and one from Ellie."

"Dad?" she said.

"He's in tribal jail, Amber. Jack says he's fine. Got a ninety-day sentence from the tribal courts."

She didn't know why that made her so sad. Nothing had changed; perhaps that was it.

"And you?"

He rolled his shoulder. "All healed up."

She stared at his face, trying to memorized every small detail, already dreading the knock and their separation.

"That's good."

"I have something else." He reached again and then presented her a legal-sized envelope which bore the great seal of the Turquoise Canyon Tribe.

"What's this?" she asked.

"They reinstated your membership. You are one of the people again."

Amber's lip and chin trembled, and the burning kept her from speech.

"I'm so sorry, Amber. I should have known. Should have trusted you."

She nodded and accepted the document, pressing it to her heart.

"They petitioned to have you returned, but the FBI and US Marshals made a strong case that you will be targeted by BEAR. They said you have information linking Harvey Ibsen to an important possible BEAR conspirator."

Theron Wrangler, she realized, though she would not utter his name for fear of endangering Carter. Instead she nodded. Carter did not press for answers, just cast her a sad smile.

"The tribe is not going to fight for your release."

She lowered her head. "I understand."

"I don't." He sounded angry.

She looked at him from beneath wet spiking lashes. Carter was glancing over his shoulder at the door.

"They'll be back any minute."

"Thank you for these," she nodded at the envelopes she clutched. "And for coming to say goodbye."

"I'm not here to say goodbye."

"What?"

He squeezed her hand. "I'm not leaving you again."

"Of course you are, Carter."

He gazed at her, and her heart thrummed in her chest. How many more seconds did they have?

"I love you, Amber. Please, be my wife."

She shook her head and retreated a step. "No. Not like this."

He tugged her hand, bringing her back to within inches. "It's the only way. Amber, be my wife."

"You'll lose them all."

"For a time, maybe."

"And maybe forever."

He kissed her, and in that kiss was the promise of everything she ever wanted in this world. Her heart twisted, and she broke away, sobbing. He hugged her, drawing her up back up against him, his mouth beside her ear.

"If you are my wife, they can't separate us. They have to take me with you into witness protection."

He turned her easily in his arms and pressed his mouth to hers in a scorching hot kiss that curled her toes. When he finally broke away the tears still flowed down her cheeks and her heart still ached, but something had changed. She had to be with him. She knew it. The cost, it pained her.

One look and she saw the love in his eyes. He could no more bear to be parted from her than she could stand to be without him. She saw the truth shining there in his eyes.

"Don't try to protect me from this, Amber, because the only thing harder than losing my family would be losing you."

"Oh, Carter!" She fell against him, clinging. "Are you sure?"

He stroked her head. "So sure."

"What do we do?"

"I have a marriage license. I have your uncle here. He'll marry us right now."

He lifted the familiar diamond solitaire from his blazer pocket, and she held out her hand. A moment later he slipped the ring onto her finger.

A knock sounded at the door. Agent Forrest appeared.

"You all ready?" he asked Carter.

"Not exactly." Carter turned and drew Amber up close to his side. "You can be the first to congratulate us."

Forrest's brows dipped, and he scowled at them. "Carter. What did you do?"

Amber smiled and extended her hand.

Forrest's ears drew back as his eyes rounded.

"My uncle is downstairs in the lobby. We want him to perform the ceremony right now," said Amber.

"And bring Jack, too. He's there with Little Falcon."

"No way."

"I need a best man. You can be our witness."

"You both have to testify," said Forrest.

Carter looped an arm around Amber's shoulder and dragged her beside him as they stared down the FBI field agent.

Forrest looked to Carter. "You know what you're doing, son?"

"For the first time in so long, I do."

Forrest exhaled. "Anything else? Flowers? Cake?"

"Yes," said Carter. "One thing more."

AMBER SAT FIDGETING beside Carter as they waited.

"What?" he asked.

"I'm afraid."

"You? I've seen you face armed gunmen and police

lineups and all manner of chaos. What could frighten you now?"

"What if, in time, you regret this? What if you grow to hate me because you had to give up your family to be with me?"

Carter slipped to his knees before her and gathered up both her hands in his.

"That will never happen. I love my family, Amber. I will miss them. But I can live without them. I can't live without you. You are my family now."

Tears of joy mingled with the tears of sorrow.

He brushed them away.

"Don't you dare feel sorry for me. This is a happy day, and I am the luckiest man alive."

Forrest returned with a brown paper bag, which he held out to Carter.

"As you requested," said the FBI agent.

Behind him appeared Kenshaw Little Falcon, followed by Jack.

Little Falcon was her mother's older brother, and they shared a high wide forehead and beetle bright black eyes. He kissed his niece, congratulated Carter and brought them together for the joining ceremony.

"One thing first," said Carter, reaching into the bag.

Jack did not look happy; in fact he looked fiercer than Amber had ever seen him, but when he saw what Carter held his eyes went wide and his jaw dropped. She'd never seen Jack Bear Den look so astonished.

Carter held a blue box. She stepped closer to get a look at the packaging that had a distinctively medical look about it. The yellow box had *DNA Harvesting Kit: Sibling Test* written in bold black letters and beneath it: *Safe, Accurate, Easy.* At the top, in small blue letters, was written: *Lab Processing Cost Included.* She straightened and looked from one brother to the next.

Carter opened the box and gave Jack a test tube, then recovered one of his own. Carter's gaze lifted to his twin.

"You sure?" asked Jack.

"Once I'm in witness protection, you can't see me. So it's now or never, brother. Get your answers. It's eating you up. I can see it. I hope this helps you find the truth." He turned to Agent Forrest. "You know how this works?"

"Just swab the inside of your cheek. Give the tube back to Jack and he can mail it out for processing."

Carter used the swab inside his cheek and returned the sealed tube to his brother.

Jack held the offering in one hand as if it were a bird's egg. Then hugged Carter with the other arm.

Little Falcon gathered them together. He spoke prayers in Tonto Apache and in English; the ceremony was short but rich in meaning.

Beside Carter as witness stood Jack and Agent Forrest. Amber longed for her sisters, but photos were taken and Little Falcon promised to get them to her family.

After the service, Carter and Amber signed the marriage license. Then the small gathering shared a toast with diet ginger ale served in paper cups.

Amber looked at her husband in wonder.

"I'm so lucky," she said, her voice cracking.

Carter kissed her again, there in a secure room in a secure facility, and she knew that she was strong enough to face what came next, because she would no longer be alone. She did not know how long they would be in protective custody. She did not know where or if they would be relocated in witness protection after the trial. But she did know that whatever came next, she and Carter would face it together.

Carter believed in her and trusted her and loved her with his whole heart.

* * * * *

When ecoterrorists threaten their home, it's up to Apache Protector, Ray Strong, to defend a young mother as they decipher the clues to their identity left by her dead father. She doesn't trust a man with a history for recklessness and he doesn't trust a woman with so many secrets, but until they discover the truth, he's her Eagle Warrior.

Jenna Kernan's
APACHE PROTECTOR: TRIBAL THUNDER
miniseries continues in February 2017
with EAGLE WARRIOR.

COMING NEXT MONTH FROM
Ⓗ HARLEQUIN®
™

INTRIGUE

Available January 17, 2017

#1689 LAW AND DISORDER
The Finnegan Connection • by Heather Graham
Dakota "Kody" Cameron never expected to be taken hostage in her historic Florida manor, especially not by men disguised as old-time gangsters searching for a fortune hidden somewhere on the grounds. Among them is undercover FBI agent Nick Connolly, who must protect Kody before she recognizes him from their shared past and compromises his cover.

#1690 HOT COMBAT
Ballistic Cowboys • by Elle James
Working for Homeland Security brings John "Ghost" Caspar home to Wyoming, far from the combat he knew as an elite Navy SEAL. Charlie McClain let go of her old flame years ago, and has been raising her daughter and tracking terrorist threats online—until her anonymity is compromised. Now reunited, Ghost will stop at nothing to keep Charlie and her daughter safe.

#1691 TEXAS-SIZED TROUBLE
Cattlemen Crime Club • by Barb Han
The O'Briens and the McCabes have a deep rivalry and get on like fire and gasoline. So when Faith McCabe's secret affair with Ryder O'Brien results in pregnancy, she keeps the baby secret and walks away. But when her half brother goes missing, Faith knows there's only one man she can turn to.

#1692 EAGLE WARRIOR
Apache Protectors: Tribal Thunder • by Jenna Kernan
Turquoise Guardian Ray Strong isn't sure how he's going to protect Morgan Hooke when he can't take her word about missing blood money for a killer her father took down. But when the young mother is targeted by an ecoextremist group, Ray realizes that Morgan may have more than clues to the missing money—she may know the identity of the extremists who paid her father.

#1693 MOUNTAIN WITNESS
Tennessee SWAT • by Lena Diaz
Julie Webb came back to Destiny, Tennessee, to get away from her estranged husband and family after an unspeakable betrayal. And maybe it's destiny that her new neighbor is Chris Downing, a police detective and part-time SWAT officer, because it's going to take all his skills to protect her when darkness from her past resurfaces.

#1694 WILD MONTANA • by Danica Winters
Both Agent Casper Lawrence and park ranger Alexis Finch know how it feels when love goes wrong. But when a grisly murder unveils a dark conspiracy in Glacier National Park, they can't fight their feelings any more than they can see just how deep the investigation will go before the truth comes to light.

YOU CAN FIND MORE INFORMATION ON UPCOMING HARLEQUIN® TITLES, FREE EXCERPTS AND MORE AT WWW.HARLEQUIN.COM.

HICNM0117

REQUEST YOUR FREE BOOKS!
2 FREE NOVELS PLUS 2 FREE GIFTS!

⬙ HARLEQUIN®

INTRIGUE

BREATHTAKING ROMANTIC SUSPENSE

YES! Please send me 2 FREE Harlequin® Intrigue novels and my 2 FREE gifts (gifts are worth about $10). After receiving them, if I don't wish to receive any more books, I can return the shipping statement marked "cancel." If I don't cancel, I will receive 6 brand-new novels every month and be billed just $4.74 per book in the U.S. or $5.49 per book in Canada. That's a savings of at least 12% off the cover price! It's quite a bargain! Shipping and handling is just 50¢ per book in the U.S. and 75¢ per book in Canada.* I understand that accepting the 2 free books and gifts places me under no obligation to buy anything. I can always return a shipment and cancel at any time. Even if I never buy another book, the two free books and gifts are mine to keep forever.

182/382 HDN GH3D

Name   (PLEASE PRINT)

Address   Apt. #

City   State/Prov.   Zip/Postal Code

Signature (if under 18, a parent or guardian must sign)

Mail to the Reader Service:
IN U.S.A.: P.O. Box 1867, Buffalo, NY 14240-1867
IN CANADA: P.O. Box 609, Fort Erie, Ontario L2A 5X3
**Are you a subscriber to Harlequin® Intrigue books
and want to receive the larger-print edition?
Call 1-800-873-8635 or visit www.ReaderService.com.**

* Terms and prices subject to change without notice. Prices do not include applicable taxes. Sales tax applicable in N.Y. Canadian residents will be charged applicable taxes. Offer not valid in Quebec. This offer is limited to one order per household. Not valid for current subscribers to Harlequin Intrigue books. All orders subject to credit approval. Credit or debit balances in a customer's account(s) may be offset by any other outstanding balance owed by or to the customer. Please allow 4 to 6 weeks for delivery. Offer available while quantities last.

Your Privacy—The Reader Service is committed to protecting your privacy. Our Privacy Policy is available online at www.ReaderService.com or upon request from the Reader Service.

We make a portion of our mailing list available to reputable third parties that offer products we believe may interest you. If you prefer that we not exchange your name with third parties, or if you wish to clarify or modify your communication preferences, please visit us at www.ReaderService.com/consumerschoice or write to us at Reader Service Preference Service, P.O. Box 9062, Buffalo, NY 14240-9062. Include your complete name and address.

HI15

Nick and Kody Cameron had passed briefly, like
proverbial ships in the night, but he hadn't had the least
problem recognizing her today. He knew her, because
they had both paused to stare at one another at the pub.

Instant attraction? Definitely on his part, and he could
have sworn on hers, too.

If Dakota Cameron saw his face, if she gave any
indication that she knew him, and knew that he was an
FBI man…

They'd both be dead.

And it didn't help the situation that she was battle
ready— ready to lay down her life for her friends.

Then again, there should have been a way for him to
stop this. If it hadn't been for the little boy who had been
taken…

Kody Cameron had a ledger opened before her, but she
was looking at him. Quizzically.

It seemed as if she suspected she knew him but couldn't figure out from where.

"You're not as crazy as the others," she said softly. "I can sense that about you. But you need to do something to stop this. That treasure he's talking about has been missing for years and years. God knows, maybe it's in the Everglades, swallowed up in a sinkhole. You don't want to be a part of this—I know you don't. And those guys are lethal. They'll hurt someone…kill someone. This is still a death-penalty state, you know. Please, if you would just—"

He found himself walking over to her at the desk and replying in a heated whisper, "Just do what he says and find the damned treasure. Lie if you have to! Find something that will make Dillinger believe that you know where the treasure is. Give him a damned map to find it. He won't think twice about killing people, but he won't kill just for the hell of it. Don't give him a reason."

"You're not one of them. You have to stop this. Get away from them," she said.

She was beautiful, earnest, passionate. He wanted to reassure her. To rip off his mask and tell her that law enforcement was on it all.

But that was impossible, lest they all die quickly.

He had to keep his distance and keep her, the kidnapped child and the others in the house alive.

Don't miss LAW AND DISORDER
by New York Times *bestselling author Heather Graham,*
available February 2017 wherever
Harlequin® Intrigue books and ebooks are sold.

www.Harlequin.com

READERSERVICE.COM

Manage your account online!

- Review your order history
- Manage your payments
- Update your address

We've designed the Reader Service website just for you.

Enjoy all the features!

- Discover new series available to you, and read excerpts from any series.
- Respond to mailings and special monthly offers.
- Connect with favorite authors at the blog.
- Browse the Bonus Bucks catalog and online-only exculsives.
- Share your feedback.

Visit us at:
ReaderService.com

HARLEQUIN®

A *Romance* FOR EVERY MOOD™

JUST CAN'T GET ENOUGH?

Join our social communities
and talk to us online.

You will have access to the latest
news on upcoming titles and special
promotions, but most importantly,
you can talk to other fans about your
favorite Harlequin reads.

Harlequin.com/Community

 Facebook.com/HarlequinBooks

 Twitter.com/HarlequinBooks

Pinterest.com/HarlequinBooks